Please return/renew this item by the last date shown. Books may also be renewed by phone or internet.

🖳 www3.rbwm.gov.uk/libraries

☎ 01628 796969 (library hours)

☎ 0303 123 0035 (24 hours)

Royal Borough
of Windsor &
Maidenhead

www.rbwm.gov.uk

**AUTHOR**
Emmanuelle Pagano was born in Rodez, southern France, in 1969. Her books have been translated into more than a dozen languages and she has won many awards for her work, including the EU Prize for Literature in 2009 and, most recently, the Prix du Roman d'Écologie in 2018. This is her second book to appear in English. The first, *Trysting*, was published in 2016 by And Other Stories.

**TRANSLATORS**
Jennifer Higgins and Sophie Lewis translated Pagano's previous collection, *Trysting*, to much acclaim. Individually, Higgins has translated numerous books from French and Italian, and Lewis's translations have been shortlisted for the Scott Moncrieff Prize and the Republic of Consciousness Prize.

MEIKE ZIERVOGEL
PEIRENE PRESS

This is a spellbinding
web of stories
about people on the
periphery. Pagano
makes rural France
her subject matter,
invoking the closeness
of a local community
and the links between
the inhabitants' lives,
but then she reminds
us how little we
know of each other.

First published in Great Britain in 2019 by
Peirene Press Ltd
17 Cheverton Road
London N19 3BB
www.peirenepress.com

First published under the original French language title *Un renard à mains nues* in 2012 by Editions P.O.L, Paris, France.
Copyright © Editions P.O.L, 2012

This translation © Jennifer Higgins and Sophie Lewis, 2019

Emmanuelle Pagano asserts her moral right to be identified as the author of this work in accordance with the Copyright, Designs and Patents Act 1988.

ISBN 978-1-908670-54-0

This book is a work of fiction. Names, characters, businesses, organizations, places and events are either the product of the author's imagination or used fictitiously. Any resemblance to actual persons, living or dead, events or locales is entirely coincidental.

Designed by Sacha Davison Lunt
Photographic image by simpleinsomnia Flickr/CC 2.0
Typeset by Tetragon, London
Printed and bound by TJ International, Padstow, Cornwall

The translation of this work was supported
by a grant from CNL – Centre national du livre

*Peirene*

*EMMANUELLE PAGANO*

*TRANSLATED FROM THE FRENCH
BY JENNIFER HIGGINS
AND SOPHIE LEWIS*

# Faces on the Tip of my Tongue

# CONTENTS

# 1

## *The Lake's Favourite*

I went to the lake every summer when I was a little girl. I lived on an arc of beach bordered by wooden fences and a forest so thick that we didn't make dens in the trees but dug them in the undergrowth instead. My uncle had built a house on this strip of shore, then a hut for tools and the pedalo, and some wonky terraces where the land sloped down to the rippling water. Near the reeds, right up close to their rustling song and their birds' nests, he had marked out a meadow where we went in search of sunshine and games. Away from these games, he had coaxed a garden into life, and my aunt picked fresh carrots there as snacks for me, the cosseted little niece. One evening, for a surprise, my uncle set a ladder against the tallest tree and hung a swing from it, but I'd always hated swings – the speed frightened me. Of the chill, taciturn lake I had no fear. I usually felt the cold, but with the lake it was different: I used to swim across it and cycle around it, and felt at home there. Swollen by the weir, its dark mass came right up to the little room whose French windows framed my nights each summer. I slept in a narrow alcove that could be closed off from the rest of the house, with sliding panels between it and the living room. We would eat there when it was too cold for noisy, open-air meals, and it was also the place for board games, homework, drawing, topping and tailing beans, and writing postcards. We did lots of things in that corner of the house, because we could sit there all crammed in together, with the spectacle of the lake before us. My aunt used to claim that there wasn't enough room in the bedrooms so I had to sleep in the alcove, and although she never said so, I know she was giving me the best holiday spot, the sofa in that recess, a nook looking almost directly on to the water.

I was the lake's favourite.

I loved my life by the lake so much that it was worth going away for a while, if only for the pleasure of coming back. The little road that led away provided just the right amount of adventure, with its blue dragonflies by day and clouds of fireflies by night. Quickly tired of walking, drawn back to the shore by the lake's magnetic force, I would return and curl up on my towel in the meadow, seeking the half-heat of siesta time and the distant company of my cousins, their cries muffled by the grasses that traced around me the shape of my body, still contained within its single-figure age. I heard them splashing mud all over their teenage suntans, discovering things in the reed beds noisy with insects and alive with water rats.

They wanted me to look at these creatures. I called them by their proper name, voles, and was proud of my precocious vocabulary, but I didn't want to touch them, no thanks. They threw me into the water to teach me a bit about life and humility. I preferred reading to playing at life and death, pretending to drown for a joke, and when they got too annoying I would drag the pedalo out to the edge of my little planet. I pedalled to the middle of the lake to read there, away from the others but not too far away. I always stayed nearby because it was there, close to the lapping of the water stirred up by their energy, close to the family teasing, that I grew up each summer.

## 2

# *The Jigsaw Puzzle*

Everyone came to see it, from down in the valleys even, they came great distances to see it. It featured in guide-books. It was so beautiful, its lines so special, it was the star of the plateau, and that bothered us a bit, my wife and me. Particularly my wife. When we'd moved into this farm, she'd raised objections to the road. I'd taken her in my arms: it's a local road, my darling, no one comes this way except on purpose, so they'd be coming to see us. And it'll be very handy for the milk van, no need for U-turns. We'd not stopped to consider the old lime tree. One of those veterans you still find here and there, fewer and fewer but still one or two, guarding the roads and outside cemeteries, squares and churches. We'd no idea that ours was so famous and so prized. Through all the years we spent here, she and I, then she and I and our daughter, we were spectators at the show. We looked on as admirers looked at the tree; we watched photographers photographing it and, more rarely, painters painting and sculptors sculpting it. As soon as the roads opened up in the spring, all those people came from down in the valleys and the town. Sometimes we were able to sell them a few cheeses, but not that often. We wondered what they were all *doing* here and we giggled at their pronouncements when the door happened to be open.

Only, my wife was upset that we were never left in peace, from the moment it was warm enough to be outside. She was sick of being disturbed while at work in her own garden, hanging out the washing, preparing the seed beds. The part of our garden on the far side of the road began there, at the lime tree. Our little girl wasn't so bothered. She was born here; she'd spent her whole life in the shade of the tree. In the spring, she had only to climb on a chair and she'd see visitors outside the kitchen window. Sometimes she even settled in the sink, just under the window, and she swore she wasn't cold there. She'd be turfed out when her smiling mother wanted to wash the lettuce. I used to joke that it was time for me to stop with the cheese-making and start charging for parking here instead.

What fascinated our little girl was all the images. She watched people's gazes, trying to work out which part of the tree interested them most, and was sometimes cheeky enough to ask for copies of their photos. She studied their different impressions of the tree, their angles, the light. She described all this to us in her childish words: here it's near, here's it far away, here it's furry. She often used to mix up furry and blurry, so the tree was furry

14

whenever there was a hint of mist or the photographer's hand was shaky. When there were no visitors, she would sit by herself picturing every possible representation of the tree – paintings, sculptures and especially photos. She'd make her own little sketches of it from every angle and in every colour under the sun.

We became friendly with one of the tree's most diligent admirers. He would come each year when the snow melted and buy our cheese and a little of our time over a coffee. One spring he came back with a box wrapped in shiny paper for our daughter. It was a handcrafted jigsaw puzzle, created from one of his photos. There were hundreds of oddly shaped pieces, all cut out by hand. Our daughter completed the puzzle I don't know how many times, especially during the winters, those winters that took so long to pass. She came to know it by heart, and sometimes she'd put it together robotically, practically with her eyes closed. We'd never really notice until the spring, and even then not every time, but during those long winters with the puzzle she was growing up. Soon it took her only two or three hours, and then just an hour, and then just a few minutes to fill in the lime tree's image. I think she stopped doing it when the tree fell. It had been dead a good while already, doubtless since before we moved into the farm, but it stood firm. It stood firm until then, until my daughter was big enough to do the puzzle in just a few minutes. One daybreak, suddenly, it was no longer there in the window. We opened the door at milking time, my wife and I, in that remnant of night that is every winter morning, and found it horizontal, a black form couched in snow that still shone grey in the dawn light. It must have fallen in the night, somehow silently, without the usual breaking and tearing that shatters a forest's silence more surely than chainsaws. We were just wondering how to tell our daughter, when she came down into the kitchen. She flew to the door with a joy that left us speechless. Her little hand fumbled at the handle; I had to help her turn it. For her, the fallen tree was no more dead than before, it was simply transformed into a tree house. It was no longer that scene above the sink which had so fascinated her, the scene from the puzzle that was now too easy; now it was a whole house to her, its enormous trunk simply awaiting all the new games our girl could devise. Amid that unexpected joy, things moved very quickly. We truly had no clue, my wife and I. We had no idea that we'd such a short time left together. We began by arguing about these new games in the tree trunk. My wife saw them as signs of unhappiness. She would say she's hiding, she's hiding because we're arguing. I'd reply not at all, we're arguing because you see distress in what is simply a game. She wanted our daughter to see a therapist, but I didn't agree. Then we argued about how we should deal with the lime tree's mourning admirers, then about everything under the sun: the price of the milk, the cheeses, the milking rota, the garden, TV programmes, the road. She'd been clear from the start, she'd never been happy to live somewhere so close to the road.

She said she'd been obliged to fence off her garden, to enclose her vegetable plot, out here in the open country, because of the people who came by road to see the tree, she who hated fences and boundaries. I replied that boundaries are the beginnings of new things.

In any case, the tree had come down – at last we would be left in peace. And indeed, we soon found ourselves alone. And then, just as quickly, we were entirely alone, not alone together but each alone, two people apart.

We separated and in the new space between us we inserted altitude and long journeys.

All of that is far away now, far in time though not in space, for I stayed, here beside the road, first with my little girl, then completely alone when she grew up, and she did grow up, even more, very fast, faster than it takes to finish a puzzle. She's at uni in a town a long way away. The tree hasn't shifted; it will lie sleeping for at least as long as it stood upright: almost four centuries, stubborn, just like us. The road regained its solitude, became like all our roads: nothing like the vast, grim motorways reaching out through the valleys; instead, with their gentle white curves marking our meadows from our moors, the little roads are like fine capillaries, running shyly and often empty. Here on the plateau I'm not the only one. Not the only one who's alone. The plateau harbours so many solitudes you might think it bustling with life. The most alone among us must be the mad old Polish man for whom my daughter has such affection, the one with the hut next to the wind turbines. He's from abroad but he seems to have been here for ever. As soon as one of the tourists up from the valleys opens the door of the shelter where he holds court, he starts spinning his far-fetched tales. A rootless guy, lost in his old age. I don't really find his stories funny; the older he gets, the sadder, more sordid and deranged they become, and I don't like to dwell on him or my neighbours, or on anyone up here, because in the end I feel even more washed up than they are.

There's nothing left in my kitchen apart from a handle on a door, the sink under the window and an old box dug out and left on the table. What fills the whole kitchen more effectively than these objects and furniture is the drifts of silence. They disperse a little when I move around, when I'm busy they get swept away, but as soon as I sit down and my thoughts turn to her, they take over the whole place again. The drifts assume the shapes of the objects and furniture – I think that's how they come to resonate in the room. I went to turn off the boiler in the dairy to let the milk calm down a bit. I've plenty of time. I sit at my daughter's place, in the chair she still takes when she comes for one of her rare visits, as if on shore leave. I open the box, I know there isn't a single piece missing; I too know it by heart and yet I haven't touched it since the tree fell. I run my fingers along the sides, the grooves of the image so carefully carved out. My land is furrowed as well: by the water, by the air. Living off the land is perhaps simply a question of deepening the channels and ridges, of hoeing, waiting and then ploughing in once more. I pick out the edge pieces first, always start with the edge pieces, and it's then that I find a few hairs among the pieces, hairs lost among cardboard sections of branches, hairs the colour of her eighth or ninth year.

# 3

## *The Short Cut*

I look so much like her, it upsets them. They think they're seeing her, seeing her returned, seeing her returning. They take me for a revenant. I've never returned, though; I haven't seen my family since then. Since I can't remember when. Actually I do know, since the death of our grandmother. They talk to me about that time when I was already another, or rather another was me, at that family wedding when a woman thought she was me, having been mistakenly invited by my cousin, the bride's mother, the one I look like, looked so much like. As though it was just like me to take someone else's place. But now my cousin is dead and they know it's actually me here, me and not another, me looking so much like her. Not her. We were almost the same age, to within a few days. We were a kind of almost-twins. I'm me now, just me. I am neither my cousin nor that ill, washed-up impostor at her daughter's wedding.

It's quite late and our shadows are long on the cemetery pathways. We walk with our backs to the sun and the shadows stretch before us, as though they were leading the procession. My cousin has preceded me to this place where shadows don't need the sun. She wanted to be cremated but her children have refused. In any case, she has already burned. She killed herself in a car accident and the car caught fire. She went up in smoke before her funeral and we haven't got much to bury. I think she decided to kill herself, I think it was on purpose. She never believed in life; despite her children and her husband, she was never alive. I knew her well before, before the husband and children, before she began to pretend. She lied herself a comfortable life, forgetting her girlhood fears, but they returned once the children were grown up, they came back, they'd always been there most likely. That's what I think, but I don't know; we'd lost touch. I think I know her better than anyone, even now she's dead. Sometimes it's as though I knew myself, because of the way the others look at me, because of those words: you're so alike you could be her. We can't know ourselves, only catch hold of words and images in other people's minds to try to see more clearly inside ourselves.

I've been around; I've lived it up, as we used to say. I'm one of the last hippies, the complete opposite of my cousin, but perhaps we were both trying to escape from the same life. The same fear of life, the same desire to live even so, but such an impossible desire, such an irresolute one. When we were teenagers she used to say she wanted to escape from this war that was our lives. I would answer that the only way to escape war was to make war. To live. I'd scarpered as soon as our grandmother died, straight from the cemetery, hitchhiking to the station. My cousin was the only one who knew about my plans, a few months before we turned eighteen. I think I threw myself into life the same way she threw her car against the crash barrier.

The paramedics found the wreck in the thickets of broom that spread their yellow scent everywhere, the roadside broom. Forget-me-nots and broom, they're not domestic flowers. Just like the forget-me-nots whose blue and pink petals we see even in the concrete high-rise outskirts of Paris, broom grows everywhere, on roadsides, even by motorways. Blue forget-me-nots were her favourite flowers. I had told her that they're called 'remember' in German and 'don't forget me' in English. I brought some to add to her grave. To give a bit of weight to the almost empty coffin. But my bouquet doesn't weigh much and that's how it should be. She said that she suffered from her own weight, or that's what her children told me. She suffered from her weight even though she was skinny, and they didn't understand that. I do. I understand. She suffered from the heaviness of a body that feels like lead when you don't want to live any more. She died light and burned up, her body nothing more than blisters and blackened air.

I'm afraid she will weigh heavily, though, in my memory, in the memories of her children and husband, and the people who will remember her. Did she think of that?

I came back specially for the funeral. Her daughter found me through the internet. I took that road again in a hire car, in the opposite direction, from the station to the cemetery. I got a bit lost after so many years, so I asked a lady the way to the cemetery and she kindly showed me a short cut. It was easy to find and I arrived in plenty of time. Something wasn't right, and it wasn't that I was early; no, it was the route I'd taken, the short cut. I was lost. I wasn't lost on the road but in my mind. It had gone too fast, this return with the short cut. The drive to the cemetery wasn't a question of time, and I didn't mind if I was late or early. This drive was a journey, with stages to be gone through in the city. The short cut avoided the city centre and its outskirts, and what we used to call the zone, the business and shopping centres, a sort of city beyond the city that frightened and fascinated us when we were children. The short cut was a country road that had brought me almost directly from the station to the cemetery. But I had stages to pass through: the city, the river at its edge, between the centre and the zone, the narrow iron bridge between the two where the city seemed to choke and where the traffic jams were all part of the journey, the zone itself, the industrial no-man's-land, the in-between places. I needed them so I could pass from one world to the other. I needed markers, segments, crossings. I needed the bridge, to pass from one reality to another, from one vision of reality to the other, from hers to mine.

I needed the return. The return to her, to us, the return to me.

I turned the car round and went back to the usual route, in the opposite direction. I arrived in her reality just as the coffin was being lowered. Just in time to fling in my forget-me-nots and light up the shadows with their little blue spots. This reality was reassuring for me, for her. I knew what frightened her most: it was the life that I had chosen where nothing is known. She had tried to persuade me not to leave, telling me that other places were the same as here but worse, because they were unknown. The unknown was what made her so vulnerable. Now we're reassured, she and I. We know where we are. She no longer weighs a thing, and I have returned.

# 4

## *Blind Spots*

I have a fail-safe technique, I promise. I stand in their blind spots. It was difficult at first. I tried lots of different approaches, refined my method. The first time I had the idea, or rather the second time, I couldn't do it. Nor the third or fourth time. I made a whole series of failed attempts. But one day I nailed it. I found myself at the bend, like the first time, because it was actually the first time: the time I didn't mean to do it. The first time I got into a blind spot it was unintentional. The bloke slammed on the brakes, he got a shock. Me too. I looked at him in our mutual alarm and he felt obliged to give me a lift. I didn't understand why he'd braked so late, why he hadn't seen me. That's what I said when I got into his car: didn't you see me there? He replied that I'd stood in his blind spot. A gap in his range of vision from inside the car. And my sudden appearance in his right wing mirror had given him the fright of his life. He said it again: the fright of my life. My death was the fright of his life.

Since then, that's where I hide, on roadsides, at junctions, invisible until one of the passing cars comes screeching to a stop. I choose my crossroads carefully. I select junctions where everyone thinks there's no point slowing down. There are lots of dangerous spots, you know, many more than we imagine. I look for the danger at each junction and, as soon as I find it, I'm right in there. I make myself invisible.

That's what I was up to, but you – you saw me, you must have, because you weren't scared. Yet I was in the blind spot – in your blind spot – I'm sure. And you were going, you are going, so fast. You're smiling. You're still going much too fast. I don't see what there is to smile about. The faster you go, the less you can see on either side. The bigger your blind spots. On the motorway it's as if we're looking down a tunnel, did you know that? You drive without seeing, seeing nothing beyond what's dead ahead. You can't see to the sides; you're blinkered. Lots of people go about with blinkers, not just on the motorways. They're not really driving their lives. I mean, not leading their lives. Instead of leading their own lives, they let themselves be carried along in their restricted view of things. Social conventions, appearances, all those things, you know, all those things that shrink your field of vision. Our vision. We don't see anything else, nothing of what's at the edges. You don't give a damn about what I'm saying. Rightly, maybe, but you're going too fast. Anyway, blinkered or not, when you drive you can't ever really look around, to the sides, at what's going on or what's there at the side of the road. You just see it in flashes. To piece the picture together, you'd have to drive past over and over again, the exact same place every time, and whatever was there, on the verge, would have to be the same, always there, the same thing always in the same place. Whatever goes on there, whoever's there, would have to be there again, not changing, hardly even moving. Say it was a man – for example, a hitchhiker or something, a loafer – he'd have to stay right there, waiting, daydreaming. Whoever it was would have to stand there every day so as to be seen. He'd wait, he'd be waiting for us, as if it were a habit, a compulsion; then, and only then, we'd be able to describe him, bit by bit, a little more each day, by passing him, going by again and again. You have to wonder who would stand there every day, waiting to be recognized bit by bit, for us to piece them together – apart from someone with a screw loose. A roadside loony. But you know, there are lots of these roadside nuts. I've come across quite a few, what with the hitchhiking. There's even one, poor sod – it's a crazy story, literally crazy: the poor thing has lost his place, he's lost his roadside. He waited there such a long time, not waiting *for* anything, just waiting, for what couldn't possibly come back, for such a long time, so long that the road moved on before he did. You're smiling, so you must be listening. He was waiting for people who'd died, can you imagine? It could've gone on his whole life. Dead people at a bend on a mountain road, he'd wait for them every day at the same time, the time of the accident. Everyone round about knew his story and made sure to let him be. That was his whole life. We got so good at letting him be that locals were in the habit of braking just before the bend, as if at an invisible sign: 'Slow down: loony'. But of course the municipal bright spark had no idea about our roadside loony. They changed the route of the A-road and the guy never found his place again. You're still smiling. That story makes me want to cry. You're untroubled. Your face looks calm. I can only see half your smile, the cheek above it, the right one, so calm too, not a twitch, no irritation. Your serenity makes you beautiful. I can't tell if you know it. Or even if you're listening. But you're driving too fast, and it's me – uncool, anything but laid-back – it's me you should be listening to. You're going too fast and, sorry, but you're driving badly. You're taking risks. Are you playing superheroes or the lady who doesn't get it? You could have killed me just now; well not quite, 'cause I took that into account, I always take it into account, precisely so I don't run any risks, 'cause, you know, I get scared too! Everyone does. But you must have believed it, must have believed you could've killed me, that's how it works. You can't have seen me. Perhaps you've got a wider field of vision, sharper eyes than the rest. You only braked afterwards, I had to run to catch up. You don't look surprised. Or rather you're still not surprised, neither by what I'm telling you nor by my being there at the junction. You worry me, you know, you're pretty but worrying. Don't tell me you're used to this kind of conversation, or to picking up this kind of hitchhiker; don't tell me you meet guys like me at every T-junction. Not a word. I'll admit: I've not met a woman like you before. So quiet and beautiful with it, so unchatty. A woman who listens to me. I think you're listening. Why you're listening, I don't know. Generally, people quickly get fed up of me and my rants. I go off on so many tangents, sometimes I even bore myself. I don't mean to flatter when I say you're beautiful. You're not the way other women are, the official beauties, the ones everyone calls beautiful. The beauties according to conventional wisdom. Your beauty is unconventional. I think you know it. I'm not trying to seduce you. I'm not after a woman. I've had it with all that. I've given a lot. Too much. You seem not to care what I'm saying, and yet you're listening. You're beautiful in your serenity, your indifference – in your difference, even. Nothing seems to reach you. If your photo were in a magazine you'd look quite ordinary, but you're not in a magazine, you're in this car that I've stepped into, you're in motion, alive, wordless and living. All the lights of the road pass over your face, these reflections and projections move over you and, I have to say it, you look so pretty. I'm talking nonsense. But you can't have seen me – and you can't have seen me and not been frightened. Perhaps that's thanks to your conscience. Maybe you have a different kind of conscience, or no conscience at all. 'Cause the trick with blind spots is you have to play on the drivers' guilty conscience. They've been horribly frightened that they might have run you over, so they take you. Especially the ones who are going too fast. So many times I've seen the remnant of recent fright in their eyes, you know? The remnant of a shock, a fright that's over, and then another fear overlaying the first: fear of me. As if I'd risen from the dead. Guilty conscience about other people. Not about themselves, though, they've got a squeaky-clean conscience when it comes to themselves; no worries there. No gaps, no blind spots, no dead ends. Then again, that's hardly possible, don't you think? We've plenty of parts that we never see and hardly know. The back of the neck, for example: we know it by touch, but seeing it is another story . . . The same with your voice: you only ever hear it inside yourself, so that's not your actual voice. The actual voice is the one other people hear, 'cause the voice is a link to other people, right? And if your true voice is the one inside you, what good is that if you're the only one who can hear it? We all have our blind spots, and plenty of 'em. All those blind spots inside us. And outside. I've always wondered why we're ourselves and not someone else. All these people around us, who see us so differently from how we are. You know what I'm talking about. It's not just voices. When I say that I've given a lot, it's because women always want to change you, to change us. They like something about us, they come up close so they can see it better, then as soon as you take them in your arms, they get used to it, they turn away, they're not so sure, they're looking for something else, something other than what they liked about you before. You don't know who you are any more. They used to assure you that you had that special thing only you had no idea of it. And then one day, just like that, the thing, that precious thing they discovered, they don't want it any more. They try to make you see yourself afresh, they get bored. You think you've changed. That thing you truly have, that irreducible thing that's deep inside, almost hidden, that true thing of yours, not what the women claimed to have found, that genuine thing, you're no longer sure you still have it. You know, that centre, that place inside that no one knows and that you'll do anything to preserve, that pristine space – suddenly it's invaded. Love and sexual relationships disturb that space, you no longer know how to be yourself, you no longer know because you have to consider someone else. You're becoming the other person. How can you be sure of being yourself? You, for example, yes you: are you sure that you're yourself? Who is really driving your car? You look at me and your smile doesn't slip but you're not actually smiling, I see it in your eyes. You don't fool me, you know. When it's just your mouth smiling, that's not really smiling, it's pretending. I'm not sure you're following all I'm saying, and I'm not sure I'm saying everything. You're here, you've picked me up, I'm here, close to you, but sitting here you seem so far away. I talk and all you do is smile. You do have a very beautiful smile – a fake one, but beautiful. Perhaps you'd rather I shut up. No: you're able to shake your head, but not to speak. So you are listening. And you tell me to go on with a nod, you don't want me to stop, for this to stop. Yes, I'm talking to you. You hardly see me when you look this way. Then did you see me in your right wing mirror? Did you see me before I popped out of your blind spot? I'm sure you didn't see me, your eyes are like everyone else's: set dead ahead. But no, you weren't afraid, and you picked me up even so. I wonder why you took me without that guilty conscience, without that fear of having killed me. Women travelling alone never take me without that fear. They don't take me because of that other fear. You know what I mean, that primal fear of being killed or assaulted: the classic fear of the hitchhiker, everyday fear, not mine, not the one I've invented with my blind-spots tactic. Fear sharpens the senses; that's also why they see me, suddenly. All the drivers were frightened, except you. It's different with you. You're the one frightening me. You're so serene, you're like my fear, you're like fear itself. Sometimes we get our fears muddled, you know. We think we're afraid of one thing and then it's something else that frightens us, as if we were frightened by proxy, at one remove. One day, a driver braked so abruptly that a layer of snow fell around my feet. I don't know where he'd come from but he had a bloody great carpet of it on his roof. He jumped out without a glance at me. I swear you'd have thought I wasn't there. He told me to move away; he walked all round his car to look at the mounds of snow scattered on the road by his sudden stop. He looked lost. I asked him what was going on and at last he looked at me, but not to apologize or explain his fear – I mean his fear of me, of course – no, he talked as if I was to stand witness. I'd testify to his snow. He'd not been anywhere it had snowed, so where had this snow come from? There were mounds of it on the ground, splatters as far as the road-side ditch, and some was still clinging to the roof, back window and front windscreen. He asked me where the snow had come from, as if I could possibly know, or as if I were the one who'd thrown it, from the blind spot where I'd been standing, who'd cast it like an evil spell, a stupid hoax, the work of a thoughtless kid aiming snowballs at cars – and in midsummer, what's more. He still took me, and all the way he went on and on about that snow.

But who are you anyway? Who are you not to be frightened – a madwoman? Now you're really smiling, and it's just as lovely, you know. You're a madwoman with a lovely smile. What am I going on about? Why aren't you frightened? Fear is the greatest human emo-tion, perhaps the only one. Even love is a sub-feeling, a by-product of fear. We love out of fear. No matter what fear, it doesn't matter. Fear of loneliness, mostly. Fear of death. Wanting to last in people's memories. Aren't you afraid of – I don't know – of disappearing? Dying? Perhaps you've taken death on wholesale, seeing as you're not afraid of it. You're some kind of ghost. Not a hint of guilt and an absolute sense of self: only death can achieve that, right? You aren't dead yet, though; you're driving this car and you picked me up. You took me with you. And I'm alive, I'm sure of it. I'm not mad. I don't want to die, I'll have you know. You drive fast and very badly, if you don't mind my saying. A pretty, mad, bad driver.

Yet you're not dead. But you're not smiling any more. I've got it, I think I've understood. In your mind, you're dead; you want to die, you want to kill yourself, is that it? You meant to kill yourself just then when you almost killed me. I'm not risking my life in those blind spots. I know how to stand just where people will think they'll hit me, but it can't ever happen. I'm safe, except in drivers' guilty consciences. You must have thought that too, so why the lack of fear? That's it, yes that's it: you wanted to kill yourself so, of course, you weren't worried about killing me. Your own death was all you could think about; you couldn't feel, you don't feel a thing for other people now. Like an anaesthetic. You're anaesthetized by your death wish; nothing can touch you any more. You're in your own tunnel, your vision is narrow, constrained by the ultimate objective, an idea so stubborn it's obscene, wretched, the singular notion of dying, whatever it takes. Dying, wanting to die, I know it's an obsession: it bends you to its will, it pins you down. This desire to die is born of a desire to live, a frustrated will to live, born of a faltering desire for life. This is the root of your fanaticism: a fault. A failure of the will to live. And now? Now I'm talking to you, you're not going to kill us, are you? You frighten me. You shake your head again, you're starting to cry. That's not very reassuring. As soon as you drop me off, you'll do it again, you'll be trying again. I can't save your life twice. You're not smiling any more, or rather you are, a little, through your tears. You're eaten up with death, through and through. Determined. A person made up of blind spots, you've lost sight of yourself, except in these sobs, this smile. You don't see yourself at all any more, what with this desire to die. But where will you go now? To the end of the world? As far as that dizzy spot, that viewpoint? You know the one I mean, the suicide point. Even though you screwed up your suicide, you'll never come back from it, not the same as before. It's a place people never altogether return from, don't you think? Have you tried before? How many times? Unless you leap from that viewpoint, unless you fly into the sublime, or into horror, it hardly matters. The end of the world isn't just an absolute, you know, it's also the place, the only place from which you have to return. No, that's not a contradiction. You never come back as you were, but you do come back. You can't go any further. The end of the world marks where you turn round. It's the place where you can't go on any more. At the world's end you have to retrace your steps; there's no other path, no alternative routes, you know that? It's not a loop, that path. At the end, you have to resign yourself to going back over old ground, on your return, over old life. It's hard work. You have to start again if you want to come home. The weariness of the same old path. You're not dead, so you have to go home. This compulsory return journey is the wearisome job of life. But it also forces you to break through to the world beyond, that of memory, the world before your death. Because you were going full steam ahead, powering through to that place at the end of the world, powering on to your death. And now you have to come back, and nothing is as it was before. That notion of death that you had, that you glimpsed, that notion of the world's end, it transforms the regions passed through on the way into a background – do you see what I mean? A backwoods. And this backwoods, this return, this has become your life: you're going back over that ground, you're on the return journey, this is where your life will be. Not steaming ahead any more – that's life too, you know. You're going to live.

The past and future always come together in the end. Here. In the present. Listen to me: perhaps you're just in the trough between the waves. It'll come back to you; we have our tides too, you know, when everything seems to recede, when we feel as though we've lost everything. We have our tides like the oceans and seas; the only difference is that our tides have no phases or calendars, and it's precisely that which makes them frightening. Look at me: I'm here, I can see you. And you know it, otherwise there'd be no crying or smiling. Look at me. I forbid you to kill yourself as long as you still know how to weep and smile. There, you're looking at me, you've seen me.

# 5

# *The Loony and the Bright Spark*

The loony and the bright spark. It could be the title of a fairy tale, a bit like 'Beauty and the Beast', a sad story with quite a happy ending. The full title would be the roadside loony and the bright spark at the construction company, but that's got less of a ring to it, for a sad story with a more or less happy ending. My story is sad too, but it has a sad ending, very sad, or rather it never ends. It starts badly, very badly, and nothing comes right, nothing is resolved. I don't actually know where it starts. I picked it up as you did, as we all did, somewhere along the road. I don't know why I call it mine; it's not my story, just one I'd like people to remember.

You probably know this guy, the roadside loony, if you live around here. You must know him if you live around here and you used to take the mountain road. But not everyone lives around here and not everyone used to take that road. In fact no one takes it any more, for a good reason. Soon no one will know this man any more, no one will remember him, and memory will do as the maps do and change his outline. Not everyone knows this man's story, and as for you, perhaps you've never even heard of him. His story doesn't go beyond this place, this mountain country where the story disappears, doesn't end, ever.

Around here, to get from one town to another you have to take roads over high passes. The towns are in the valleys and the roads plunge and climb, always winding around the verticals. They are wide and sinuous, and no one's afraid of the bends. We drive along them quite quickly, confidently. I used to take the mountain road to work. And to come back from work, of course, but it's never quite the same in the other direction. It was on the way back that I saw him, suddenly, as we all did. We each took him by surprise the first time, or rather we were taken by surprise, and almost every time it was evening. I braked when I saw him, as I was driving downhill. For some of us it was a little less accidental. Some people saw the cars slowing down, braking or switching on their hazard warning lights before they saw the man himself. Because that's the habit we got into, all of us, after the surprise of the first time, a tacitly shared habit of slowing down and warning those behind, before we even saw him, just before we got to his place. His place was there, before, at a bend in the road: always the same spot, always at the same time. His place was an evening ritual. Waiting. His place was a moment. Waiting for a lifetime, his body propped against the crash barrier.

Never behind it, which would have been safer, but – but no one hit him. In the end everyone knew, everyone slowed down as though an invisible sign had warned them of the danger.

I say in the end, but that's misleading because there's no end to this story, as I said. He's still waiting, but he no longer has anywhere to wait. He's lost in the mountains, wandering and unhappy. He was already unhappy, and already wandering too, but he only wandered in his head, in his place there, at the roadside. In his moment. Safe despite everything, even though he was standing in front of the barrier instead of behind it. Safe because we knew him, we slowed down, we had the 'Slow down: loony' sign in our heads. It flashed through our routines, our everyday journeys. We switched our warning lights on. That place that was his at the end of every day around five o'clock was the opposite of a place for us, the non-loonies. For us it was a question. For him it was knowledge. A landmark in a life of things turned upside down, of waiting. A life entirely turned towards the impossible, the inversion of paths taken, backward turns. He waited there for things to be reversed, for the past, for the return of the dead. Going backwards every evening at about five o'clock, waiting for life to be different.

For those, like me, who were driving down at that time, he was very close, on the right-hand verge, the side of the ravine. We were the most careful. For those going up, he was on the other side of the road and some didn't see him, caught up in their bend and their return home.

We would all come up with answers to the question of what he was doing there, but I don't know if they were really answers. The man was one of those people who 'haven't their peace'. That's how we describe them around here, our loonies. He worked at the social enterprise down in the town. He lost his peace by the side of the road one evening at about five o'clock when his wife and children were killed on the bend going down, more than forty years ago. They were taken by one of those easy-as-pie hairpin bends on our mountain roads. More than forty years without anyone redoing the road, without re-routing it, we should have expected that at some point the engineers would get involved.

We didn't see it coming, the diversion project, and yet I know now, because I looked into it afterwards, that you don't change the route of a road from one day to the next, just like that. There are studies that take years, with a whole heap of things for the bright spark at head office to take into account. The plan goes through a series of processes, refined with each new dossier, from the initial idea to the detailed project. First it considers how the road, this artificial element, will integrate into the natural environment. The construction must be solid and stable, built to withstand exterior elements and internal forces. Then there is the more functional aspect to be considered: all constructions must have the right geometric design and surface condition to ensure the smooth and safe flow of traffic transporting people and goods. All that is very rational and so vast, compared to our little sad story. Little, sad, but never-ending. There's more than engineering in the creation of a road; there's something more complex, something we cannot grasp. A flux that is about to be fixed down. Written. That will be drawn. Printed. There are politics and economics within it, in the attempts to find the project that will have the widest reach for the lowest cost. There are the environmentalists too, and the residents, apparently the residents are taken into account. But no one has ever put any questions to us. Let alone him. Maybe to you they have. Apparently they take into account the impact of the infrastructure on the regional amenities, trying to respect the way of life and integrate into the landscape. This man, this man was a sort of landmark in the landscape, a silhouette of waiting, a man-comma who told us, with his hunched body, we're here, at a particular place, it's five o'clock. A shadow dial on the bend. I don't exactly know who decides, but no one saw it coming.

They put the construction site further up the hill, and I don't know how he knew but he knew, before we did, and he climbed up to see what was happening. The site was no longer a site for re-routing the road, but a space made to mark out this man. None of the workmen dared throw him out or disturb him. He didn't disturb them, and he was disturbed enough already. The barriers came up like a frame, the mesh like little close-ups; all the structures of the building site were strokes underlining him and the temporary traffic lights were spotlights to pick him out.

And under these lights, within these lines, he was unrecognizable.

We had only known him in fragments, in little bits, but we began to see him in his entirety when the building began. It was when we had to stop at the traffic lights, right next to him. In front of him. Face to face. Now we would stop up close and we could see his madness in its entirety. Before, because we were driving, we only had pieces of him, seen in passing, stolen each time we slowed down, bits of him that we assembled mentally and that eventually became the figure we all talked about and thought we knew, on the strength of so many journeys and memories. A sideways figure, broken like a comma pinned to the crash barrier, the barrier that hadn't been there on the day of the accident, the barrier that had become the line, the border, the safeguard. He stood next to it in danger, on the roadside, always around five o'clock and always in the same position. The barrier was his prop, his story began with it. It had been put up after the car crashed, the car that never came home to him, that he was still waiting for. Because he was there every day – same time, same place – we had this strange opportunity to look at him in bits, one piece of the figure every day, until we knew him by heart: his unchanging habits, his uncertain but clearly quite advanced age, his slumped body, his careless gaze protected by an old ski mask. We thought we knew them, him and his story. Him and his waiting, him and his long comma body.

And yet multi-criteria studies to re-route a road, economic strategy, site layout, safety, the number of accidents avoided per year, the number of deaths avoided per year, the number of serious injuries avoided per year, advantages for users, time, hours gained, running costs, a favourable, neutral or unfavourable environment, the initial situation, the number of obstacles, risks of interruption to traffic, the number of safety black spots, impact on employment, the number of jobs linked to the investment, upkeep and operation, energy, energy efficiency, energy performance, impact on other modes of transport, variation in revenue for competing modes, financial cost to public authorities, economic investment cost, overall economic cost, variation in tax revenue, balance of cost versus monetizable benefit, calculated overall benefit, actual profit, calculated profit, immediate rate of return, all those things he talked about, the bright spark at head office when I went to warn him, all that is nothing compared to the complexity of our roadside loony. This tormented waiting that we can't comprehend, this disaster, it's him, it's what's inside his head, it's the whole of him that we thought we knew but that goes beyond our knowledge. He goes beyond the figure we made of him, that we thought we could reduce him to. He escapes from the story in which we paraded him. He is irreducible, he can't be explained or understood, even if we put together all the fragments of him lingering in the memories of all the drivers.

We saw the big sign explaining the re-routing around the mountain. I took it upon myself to go and warn the site staff, but they didn't want to hear it. Our loony stayed on the building site right until the end, silent and obdurate, never straying from the huts along the new road. He moved with them, stayed within their structures. First teasing, then gentle, the workers soon got used to him. Some passed him food through the barriers. The people from social services would come and lecture him, try to take him away, but he came back every day.

When it was all finished, he didn't go back to the hostel, he didn't return to the old road as we hoped he would, he didn't go back to his ritual. A road without cars? We must have taken him for an imbecile. How could his family drive back along a road where cars no longer passed? He followed the new road. Then another, then another. And another. He's looking for his bend, his moment, his watch. We've passed him several times, at the side of different roads, never standing still, never leaning against the crash barrier, never sitting down, never immobile. He who was never straight but always hunched into a comma on his bend, bound to his time, no longer bends. He no longer stoops. He no longer waits – he doesn't know what time it is. He walks without pause along the roads around our mountain, and for a few weeks now we've lost sight of him completely.

# 6

## Mum at the Park

On Sundays, I always wanted to go to the park in town with Mum. She preferred going to the river, not to the sunbathing parts but to places that only a few people knew about, peaceful places. I didn't want peace, though. I wanted to kick a ball around with my friends. A peaceful place, for my mother, meant somewhere she could read. She never used to play with me, she barely even talked to me, just as she barely talked to anyone, except when necessary, except, just sometimes, to her children. I was the youngest of the three, the little boy who still needed to play.

Mum didn't like the park because of the people. Not simply because they were there, not simply because she always wanted to be alone, but because the people in this park were worse than other people. They were dirty and raucous, aimless and hard to shake off. All the poor people, so poor they didn't even have a driving licence, let alone a car, drifted to this park on Sundays, gravitating towards a very big old lime tree surrounded by graffiti-scrawled benches. There were lots of spelling mistakes on the wooden benches, but not on the seemingly indestructible bark of the tree, and, rushing around the benches, jumping over them and squirming underneath them, there were always plenty of children. I liked that, and Mum wanted me to be happy, so we went there, abandoning the calm of the water and the riverbank, leaving behind the regular, comforting sounds of the current, the rustle of pages and the echoes of my solitary football. Mum always said yes in the end. She would sit down beneath the tree, holding orphaned in her hands a book she knew she wouldn't be able to read, but with the pleasure of seeing me smiling and playing with the other children.

On that particular Sunday there were lots of children with their dubious-looking parents, but also quite a few younger people without children, sprawled comatose on the benches, finishing off their night out in the middle of the afternoon in the lime tree's shade, guarding their dogs and their beers with their feet. I could see the fearful, fed-up look on Mum's face as she sat down as far from them as possible. One of them, awake, bored and already tired of life, started trying to chat her up. She replied politely that she wanted to read, and she did actually start to read, once she had encouraged me to get the balls out of the bag (a basketball and a football) and to go and introduce myself to the other children, who were also laden with balls and on the lookout, like me, like everyone, for new friends. But I wanted to talk to Jérémie. He had just introduced himself, holding out his suntanned hand, so I knew he was called Jérémie. He looked about the same age as my older brother, and Mum pointed this out. I've got a son your age, you know. He looked nice and he looked canny. He'd already worked out that if he wanted to seduce my mum, he had to win me over. He started to explain dribbles and passes to me, all sorts of things about football and basketball, and even lots of things that had nothing to do with football or basketball, things sport could teach us about life: altruism, respect, team spirit, playing straight, sticking to the rules, getting along with others. And at the same time he told me about his own life, a life that was already slipping by, the abandoned sports studies diploma, the job he claimed to have as a sports coach, his problems. I could tell he was talking to Mum, really, but in just a few minutes he'd become my best friend in the whole park.

Mum was trying to focus on her book, checking on me once in a while as subtly as possible so that Jérémie couldn't catch her eye. Whenever he did manage to, he'd begin reeling off heavy-handed compliments about the blue of her eyes, that blue she had passed on to me, undiluted, a blue bluer than the river on a sunny day, the blue of a cloudless winter sky, astonishingly bright in her ageing face, worn by time and sadness. I was a bit jealous but only a bit, because I knew I was her favourite. I knew he didn't have a chance, and I made the most of his loneliness to play with him, because she never wanted to play with me.

She had used up all her patience with my brother and sister and I don't think she could stand any more ball games. She could only stand books and walks. She loved being with me and going for walks with me. She loved me. She just didn't love the town, or the people in town, or the dirt in the streets and the park. Mum came from the countryside and always talked about how she longed for the moment when she could go back there, which irritated my older sister and me because we loved being here, near the shops and the rough part of town, the basketball hoops and the goalposts. Our brother lived in an even bigger town which seemed a dreamland to us, or a fantasy land, as Mum said.

When she was young, she didn't play the same sorts of games as we did. She daydreamed among the trees, did jigsaw puzzles without getting bored, spent lots of time drawing and already read a lot. She lived alone with her dad in such an isolated place that it took hours to go and visit her mum. It was so far from the city crowds that you could tell when one of your neighbours was passing just by listening for the sound of them walking in the snow, counting the number of steps by the dry, tearing sounds, shocking in the silence. Mum used to say that silence doesn't exist, that there are always tiny sounds in the background, muted and barely perceptible. And she was an expert in barely perceptible things. Her whole childhood was made up of them. Mum had red, prematurely aged hands, as if she'd been a cleaner, a labourer or a farmer, but she hadn't done any of those things. She just took so little care of herself, her hands, her face, anything to do with her appearance, so little care that it was almost a bit strange, as though she wanted people to think she was someone else. I gazed at her hands holding the book and missed a pass from Jérémie. His little dog started barking and jumping around like a mad thing.

My distraction was driving the puppy mad with excitement, as though each kick I missed pressed a button on a remote control linked to his tiny body, and he kept rushing after the lost ball, a noisy bundle of energy. I followed this joyful little dynamo, forgetting Mum for a minute or two, but when Jérémie started telling me how his dog had picked up the scent of a fox the day before, as it was nosing through the bins, I turned to her straight away with a knowing smile. When she was a little girl, Mum had killed a fox with her bare hands to put an end to its suffering. She had often told us about this memory and, more often still, we'd asked her to tell the story again and again. It seemed a miracle to me that a fox could stray into town, like a reconciliation with Mum. She looked at me and returned my smile, but with a finger to her lips to say that we should keep that story in the family. I felt the same. She took a snack out of her bag for me. She never forgot the snacks or the water or the books. Or even the balls.

\*

I ran over to sit next to her, and Jérémie made one last attempt to get Mum's number, gave us a carton of apple juice, then finally said goodbye. He woke his friends and whistled to the dogs. They all left without closing the gate and as they went out another dog came in, an old white dog with wobbly hind legs. He didn't have any of the bounce or playful barks of a young dog, but that didn't stop him chasing after the ball with me once I'd finished my sandwich and Mum had picked up her book again.

# 7

# *The Automatic Tour Guide*

I'm waiting for the automatic tour guide to die.

It would be a blessed release, to tell the truth. For us and for him. It pains me to see him now. He's not as popular as he was in the old days, when tourists used to come just for him, for the guide, and the gîte was booked up months or even a couple of years in advance.

He isn't a guide, he's more of a storyteller, an automatic storyteller. Perhaps we should have called him the automatic raconteur, but because he's sometimes more like a geographer-geologist-historian or a guide for armchair hikers, pointing out the paths his stories take, we've always called him the automatic tour guide.

His name is actually Ukalo.

It's January and the lady from social services keeps going on at me. We won't be able to leave him where he is for another whole winter or they'll come and put him in a home. Still, I'm not that worried, because I'd be surprised if he lasts much longer, what with all the trouble we had with him last winter and him refusing to leave the shelter. If only he'd let us do it up a bit, build proper walls, insulate it or something, but he's stubborn, like all the old people from these parts, even though he isn't really. I mean he isn't really from these parts. He's definitely old. And stubborn. Won't admit he can't look after himself any more, so we just have to watch him fading away and wait for him to drop down dead.

Better to have him drop dead here than put him in a home.

I take his lunch every day. He goes home and waits for my Tupperware. In the evening he manages by himself, making soups with vegetables from the garden or from tins. It gives him something to do until the news comes on.

The gîte isn't like it used to be and we often get people who don't know about him. They don't come for the automatic guide, they come for the drama of the panoramic views, or just for the shrill, brutal air of the plateau, for the blue-shadowed snow on very cold days, for the autumn blaze of the maples, the great daubs of green in summer. Some end up in the area more or less by chance and the tourist office sends them along without warning them.

They're surprised, that's for sure, and sometimes taken aback.

This week's guests haven't opened the back door once and they're leaving soon, before midday. Ukalo is taking it badly. He hasn't said anything but his silence is hard to bear and I've been worrying all week, wondering whether they were going to open the door or not. They're packing their bags now, going back and forth dirtying the snow with their feet, loading their stuff into the squeaky-clean 4x4.

This whole week I've kept an eye out, not making it too obvious and not hanging around too long either, because it's bloody freezing. I've seen Ukalo sitting so close to the fire he could have burned himself, poking the embers with his battered stick, crushed by the waiting. I think he's been going over all the tales and legends in that leaky head of his, to pass the time and improve his performances, and to compensate a bit for the sudden memory lapses. It's perfectly normal, given his age, but for an automatic guide it's a blow. He invites us over to have coffee with him nearly every day, and when he goes blank in front of us, when he opens the door and forgets why we're there, I see him disappear from behind his face, and that wrinkled face is like a fallow field, useless.

Sometimes he makes it into a joke, and with the imagination he's got, he comes out with all sorts of funny reasons for it. Bizarre excuses for the gaps in his memory. Oh, I went out into the garden, you know, and as I bent down to pull up some carrots, I lost track of time. But where? In the garden, in the ground. I got lost on the path up to Tendrier because of the ultrasound. You know, the ultrasound from the wind turbines. Ukalo, the turbines don't make ultrasonic waves, and anyway, only animals and children can hear them. That's it, I got lost because I was looking for somewhere I could hear them, looking for the time, the time when I was young. I was wondering where the hearing I had when I was twenty could have got to. When he's like that, full of forgetfulness and ideas, a wink and a smile at the ready, we find ourselves wishing the gaps in his memory were even wider, so we could listen to him fill them with captivating stories. But not in winter, never then. Sometimes in winter I suddenly realize he's gone out in the middle of the night and I run after him, not even putting my jacket on. I find him out there in the moonlight, sitting in the snow lit up bright as day, and I shout, When are you going to get on with it and die? I scream like a crazy woman, my head pounding from the cold and from running around in my nightie.

I don't want him to die, because I'm very fond of him, more than just fond. But a life like that, well, I'm not sure it really is a life, and that's partly our fault also. I feel ashamed, even though I keep telling myself it's better than a home or the mental hospital, and my husband and I are sick of social services breathing down our necks, so we're just waiting for it to be over, all the while making money from the tourists he attracts.

My husband says it's no way to treat someone, and that we're going to end up in trouble with the Farmers' Mutual because we can't declare our automatic tour guide. His papers went out of date decades ago. We do wonder what the police are waiting for, with everything you see on the news about families being sent back, but not him, oh no. They know him and they know full well what the situation is, and yet they've never come knocking. We're not above board and that bothers my husband. We often argue about Ukalo, like we used to argue about the children, but worse because we haven't got the patience we had when we were young.

The social services lady comes to check on him every so often and I see her glancing around to check that the place is clean and Ukalo is decently dressed. At the slightest sign of neglect it'll be off to the home with him. I wonder how they'd manage it, given that he's not even legal. But I'm not worried about that. The house is neat and Ukalo looks well turned out. He's always been very meticulous.

His house is tiny, just one room on the ground floor and a bedroom with a little washroom upstairs.

It's connected to our gîte by this shelter where he does his automatic guiding. The shelter's open to the elements and our grandchildren tried to give Ukalo the nickname 'bats in the belfry', because the wind whistles all around him and because he's going batty. But the name never stuck; Ukalo's the automatic guide, not the village idiot.

My husband and I live on the other side of the gîte and our top floor overlooks the shelter. That's all there is of our little hamlet, these few buildings.

*

All the buildings belonged to our grandparents and our grandfather's brother, my great-uncle, who was a bachelor his whole life and was always just known as 'Uncle'. It was Uncle who brought Ukalo here in the 1950s. I was very little and my sister had just been born. Uncle was over forty and he must surely have known that having a foreigner on the farm wouldn't attract a woman there, quite the reverse. His older brother, our grandfather, had about ten children and lots of grandchildren already, so that would be enough. A woman was more expensive than a foreigner, and a foreigner would be a better worker than a woman.

We had a shortage of farm labourers. The Polish had a shortage of everything. Uncle lived in Ukalo's house. Or, well, the other way around, the opposite really, but anyway. Ukalo came to live in Uncle's house, in his bedroom. They had two single beds and were almost the same age. Ukalo and Uncle lived their bachelor lives together like two room-mates, communicating in Uncle's language, a patois that I could never understand, a sort of Occitan peppered with family words, invented by the family and for the family, a blood language that wasn't passed down beyond Father's generation and that only Ukalo still speaks today. He hasn't got anyone to speak it to, so he doesn't use it much, just a few words here and there in automatic mode for the fascinated tourists. He and Uncle shared their little world of words and habits until Uncle died about ten years ago. The old man left his house to the labourer, his friend, his foreign brother, his Ukalo, as he used to call him.

My parents had already taken over the farm after my grandparents died, Father being the only one of their ten kids to accept the slavery of the fields.

It wasn't long before it drove him to suicide, after he'd let my little sister be scattered all over the pumpkin field. Mother waited until I was eighteen, seeing as I was the only one left after my sister died, before finally giving in to cancer. We divided everything up and I was the only one who wanted to stay with Uncle and Ukalo, me with my scatterbrain, my husband and my three children. My husband worked nearby, so it was convenient really.

When Uncle died, our three children had already gone off to their new lives, city girls and proud of it. We'd just started renting out the gîte to give ourselves something to do. By then my husband was retired from the postal service and I had no more children to look after, or even any animals, just the housework in the gîte every Saturday, so my brothers and sisters didn't give it a second thought. I was the one who'd look after Uncle's heir.

The whole family was there on the morning of Uncle's funeral, my brothers, sisters, aunts, uncles and cousins, but they were all gone again by the evening. We couldn't have put them all up here in any case. Ukalo came to our house for a coffee. He watched them getting ready to go, muttering in his language or perhaps in Uncle's language, like he always does when he wants to say something without saying anything, when he wants to be heard without being understood – or the opposite, I'm not sure. He put the cup down on the tablecloth, taking an age to open his big hands, as though it were impossible to let go of the coffee cup. Then, very quickly, decisively, he got up without saying a word, not even in his or in Uncle's language. He left and went over to Uncle's house, or his house as it was now. He stopped to say hello to the guests who'd just arrived at the gîte. They were the brazen sort and, while there was nobody around because we were all at the funeral, they'd managed to open the gîte's back door, which gives on to the shelter in front of Uncle's house. Ukalo stood there surprised and silent as they replied to his hello and started telling him how much they liked our part of the world, the plateau, being on holiday, and then all about their lives, and blah blah blah. Ukalo sat down on the little bench in the shelter and he started talking too, about everything and nothing, about the fox that a little girl had killed with her bare hands in January, our latest little news story, then about Uncle, my little sister and people from the village who were dead now. There was no stopping him, and there were certainly plenty of dead people to talk about, more than there were living ones. Ukalo talked as if he were reading aloud, with an expressionless, rhythmical delivery, already in automatic mode, and those rude tourists closed the door, saying, Right, we're off for our dinner, bye, thank you, but still it wasn't a very polite thing to do, if you ask me.

*

Ever since that evening, since Uncle's funeral, Ukalo has been the automatic tour guide. At first we tried our best to make him stop. We didn't want him bothering people. But Ukalo would spit on the ground with rage every time I tried to intervene. We ended up letting him get on with it.

Whoever's staying in the gîte has only to open the back door any time between eight in the morning and midday, and then again from one to five, and Ukalo will begin his stories, not letting anyone reply or comment. You open the door and he talks, and to make him stop, you have to close the door.

He does the guiding every day except Sunday, because he's a Christian, but mainly because he doesn't want to miss 'The Sunday Phone Call' on Christian Radio France. Sometimes he'll skip Mass without complaining if I can't be bothered to drive him down to the village and wait for him in a bar with a book, because, personally, if I've got to sit through a load of old twaddle I'd rather it was in a book than in church. But I haven't always got a book on the go, so one day we agreed that we'd go to Mass about once a month, that was plenty, and he didn't grumble, not in his language or Uncle's, or even ours. But as for missing 'The Sunday Phone Call', no chance. He can't do without it. It's a kind of obsession, or a kind of food, like air and water, a bit of time all to himself. It's a programme where people call in and leave a message for family members in prison, via the radio. Ukalo is addicted to it. He moves right up close to the radio with his mouth open, listening greedily. He sits there hoovering up all the messages so eagerly, inhaling them through his mouth, that I sometimes wonder if he's done time in prison back home, or if he feels as though he's in prison here, in his shelter. It's as though he's expecting a message from someone, maybe from his family in Poland, or from Uncle, speaking from beyond the grave via CRF, like a good stupid Christian. If he thinks he's going to find them all in heaven, Uncle, Father, Mother and my little sister, then he's just as thick as the holidaymakers who stand listening by the back door, thinking that what he's saying is genuine local folklore. As if.

Often the tales he tells aren't authentic legends, and it isn't just that they're made up, they're not even from around here. They're Ukalo's stories, things that he's found in old newspapers, not quite a hundred years old but not far off. He weaves them all together and adds bits of his own memories from Poland, spices them up with some family patois and sticks in a few local place names to make them sound bona fide. I caught him at it one evening. He was reading his tatty newspapers, completely absorbed, looking for who knows what on dog-eared old maps, and looking inside himself too, I think. He had a glazed expression, as though he was peering into the cracks in his memory. He looked drunk, sitting there at the table with his head in his big, shaky hands and papers scattered around him on the tablecloth in a huge mess. He was embarrassed and tried to convince me that he'd got the newspapers out to peel some vegetables, but he hadn't picked any vegetables that day and yesterday's soup was already heating up on the wood stove. He couldn't fool me. It was the papers themselves, and his whole life along with them, that he was peeling to replenish his stock of stories.

My little sister's death doesn't need inventing, and when he tells it to the people staying in the gîte he doesn't embellish it with local colour. He delivers it straight, raw, hardly like a story at all.

For a few months now, in spite of all the coffees, medicines and glasses of water that I make him drink, he's been getting more and more dehydrated. The inside of his mouth hurts because he hasn't got enough saliva. When he wants to speak, he constantly has to open and close his mouth, and his lips make a series of rapid, regular sounds, slightly moist clicks like a suckling baby.

It was to the accompaniment of these delicate lapping sounds that I heard him recite the story of my sister's death yet again, just over a month ago, as I was closing the shutters on the early December darkness. It was nearly five o'clock. He was telling it to the latest person to open the door, a boy come to have a fag in the bitter cold. No doubt it was a good excuse to give his parents: popping out for a quick smoke before the automatic guide knocked off for the day. He was shivering hard, caught unawares by the sudden, savage nightfall that we have in these parts, when the air shines with a cold that catches you by the throat and when you feel as though each breath is tearing at your insides. I don't know if the cigarette made this feeling worse or better but, with touchingly awkward embarrassment, he asked if he could move closer to him, to the guide, and to the fire. Ukalo carried on with his story, told to the rhythm of the baby-like suckling sounds, without replying, in his usual mad, obsessive way. The boy sat down next to him, the cigarette a red spot in the blue of the snow streaked with ash plumes. I'd just closed the shutters on the top floor and didn't want to hear any more. I knew what happened next. I heard it despite myself, as if Ukalo's voice, so thin and age-worn, as if this voice deformed by the sucking of words seeking water, as if this diminished voice, reduced to incessant blinks of sound, as if this parched voice could travel so far and penetrate the shutters and double glazing of the window where I rested my forehead.

I know what happened next. Father left the tractor in the pumpkin field just behind the house without bothering to take off the rotary tiller, annoyed at being interrupted in the middle of preparing the seed beds, and ran towards the house to answer the telephone. Mother had come out to the doorstep, my sister and me clinging to her skirt, and was waving her arms to tell him to come and take the call. He came in with his boots still on, cursing Mother. She followed him once she had detached us from her legs.

My sister ran off towards the tractor but I didn't, I knew we weren't allowed, and I told her not to but she didn't listen, that little two-year-old silly. Father came out again almost straight away, still cross, went back to the field and got on the tractor. He started it up again, and when he heard me screaming louder and higher than the sound of the engine, when he felt the tiller jam, he was really beside himself, absolutely furious this time. He stopped the engine, he jumped out of the cabin like a madman, telling me to shut it. He went round and bent down to disengage the tiller. He stood up again immediately. He came back to the house and I was running behind him, I overtook him. Mother was on the doorstep again, immobile and grey, rooted to the spot, as though she were made of cement and stupefaction. I grabbed on to her. Father shoved past us and went straight to the cupboard for his rifle. I remember I ran to Uncle's house and straight into Ukalo's arms when Mother collapsed.

The tourists at the gîte came to say goodbye and thank you. They went off in a sparkle of frost and a gleam of bodywork, and there was so much glitter in their going that it brought tears to my eyes. They hadn't once opened the back door.

It's past midday and Ukalo is still sitting in the shelter. He must have lost track of time. I go to him and bend down to give him the Tupperware. He hasn't invented some convoluted, fantastical reason for forgetting what time it is. He gets up with a new heaviness and without looking at me he goes back inside.

I'm cold. I go home when I hear the lonely bing of the microwave.

# 8

## *Just a Dad*

When I was a little girl I had to see a therapist because I'd killed a fox with my bare hands. I was happy to go along with it, but I never really saw the therapist because he always had his back to me, and in any case it wasn't all that bad, the thing with the fox, or at least it was bad but I thought I was doing the right thing. It was caught in a trap and couldn't get away. It was dying, and I just pressed its neck hard, crying the whole time, to make it die more quickly. To loosen the snare of sobs that was choking me.

My parents had just separated, and then there was the business with the fox, and my age, nine, so there was no getting round it: off to the shrink for me.

Mum was annoyingly keen on arranging everything just right. She was frighteningly well organized and the therapist was the same, so between them they worked out a way of getting the most from our journeys back and forth. Dad had stayed high up in the mountains, where we all used to live together when everything was still all right, and Mum had moved down to the bottom, to a village in the valley where the weather was milder. I lived with Dad during the week, and every weekend it felt as though I was swapping seasons. On Fridays after school, Dad took me to Mum's house, and Mum drove me back up on Sunday evenings. I'd be reunited with the winter, and with my dead tree, the one that fell down shortly before the divorce and that I used to play in until dusk, and sometimes long after. I'd made a den in its huge trunk. That tree had been famous for a while. Someone had even written a book about it. When the therapist called to fix a time for my appointments, he mentioned that he drove up to see another child in a village halfway along the mountain road on Fridays, so Mum seized on that straight away – couldn't they meet there, my dad and my therapist, halfway, and make use of the journey? He would pick me up in that village and the session would take place in the car, as we drove down to Mum's house.

The therapist was a transition between Dad and Mum, and I really didn't like the way he drove, not a bit. He used to pick me up as arranged, at the midpoint, and I'd be worrying about all the twists and turns in the road before we even set off.

We would talk without looking at one another. There I was, imprisoned in the car seat, held fast by the seat belt, telling his back all about my misfortunes. As we wound along the mountain road a slight nausea permeated my words. The therapist wasn't a good driver and he didn't negotiate the bends as well as my parents did. The downward plunges frightened me. And anyway, being in the car with a man who was almost a stranger driving in front of me brought back bad memories of a time when I'd been afraid, so horribly afraid that I forgot to be afraid of the scolding that would follow.

The fox was grey. That winter had been extremely cold and the fox had a very thick coat with long, almost white hairs on the outside and a thick, much darker, downy layer underneath, like a sort of warm shadow. It had stopped struggling when I found it and had wrapped itself up in its thick winter tail as though to sleep, but it wasn't sleeping, it was dying. It gave off a strong smell of urine and violets, as all foxes do, but this smell went far beyond the usual flowery whiff. It was the smell of panic. The smell was what led me to it. Apart from that, it was just a grey hollow in the snow. When I lifted it up I saw that its body was black with blood underneath, where the snare had sunk deep into the flesh. It tried to bite me, but so slowly that I could tell it was already far gone. Gone beyond fear, just waiting. But this just waiting was horrible. I held it to me and felt the faint beating of its heart. I couldn't manage to loosen the snare, which sliced straight through my gloves, and anyway I didn't want to free it; it was too late. I tried to use the metal wire to finish it off but it was impossible. I took off my shredded gloves and strangled it with my bare, frozen hands.

Before I did it, I stared at my gloves for a long time. They weren't gloves any more, just padded tatters. I wasn't afraid of what Dad would say, not at all, but I couldn't tear my eyes away from these rags, torn to shreds like the fox's coat. And my hands too, I looked at my hands, bizarrely white and intact. The fingers of my gloves were damaged but I was unscathed. I just had cold hands; my hands, fingers, palms, nails, wrists, all were smooth, firm, pale and naked. I looked at my torn gloves and my ungloved hands. My bare hands.

I put them on the fox's neck as though to warm them, or to warm it. I squeezed as hard as a girl my age could.

Seeing the therapist always reminded me of the moment I'd been most frightened in my whole life. That moment wasn't the one with the fox. It wasn't even in winter. It was a simple, summer fright, on a very hot day. The summer I turned six, a man picked me up in his car. He was looking for the police station and I knew where it was because my grandad was a policeman. I was in the village with Granny and had let go of her anxious hand. The man came up to me. I don't know what came over me, but I suddenly forgot all the well-worn phrases that Granny, Mum and Dad used to recite about not talking to strangers. I'd never really known what a stranger was. I didn't know what one would look like, how old he'd be, what sort of clothes he'd wear. So I wasn't suspicious of this one because I didn't know he was one. I got into his car with him so I could show him the way more easily, and

I wasn't scared until he suddenly jammed the brakes on in front of the police station and asked me to get out, just in case people thought . . . I looked at him and realized what could have happened. I started to panic as I undid my seat belt, and I ran all the way to my grandparents' flat.

The therapist was looking for a link between the fox and the stranger. I thought he was stupid. It was he who was like the stranger: I didn't know him but there I was, sitting just behind him. Every Friday I sat behind the stranger, every Friday I got out of the car at my mum's house while the stranger sat at the wheel. He was a bad driver. It made my stomach churn. Ups and downs inside me. For a therapist, he wasn't very good at analysing things. He kept saying that he wasn't a stranger, that I did know him. And then in a different voice he would say that I still hadn't told him anything about the fox. I never replied. He would ask if the fox was a symbol of fear and if I knew what a symbol was. I would just smile and then (and it was exactly like this, every Friday) he would start to talk about my parents, about their separation, and my rather wild, isolated life with my dad. The fox, the symbol and Dad. In that order. But the fox's fear wasn't my fear. It was the fox's. The fox was afraid, not me. One day I'd really had enough and I suddenly asked him, right in the middle of telling the story of the summer I spent with Granny and Grandad when I was six, whether he'd noticed the roadside man. We'd just driven right past him. I asked if he'd seen him waiting for his dead to return, there on the bend, leaning against the safety barrier. The therapist said he was harmless, that everybody knew him and that I shouldn't be scared of him. I should stop going on about strangers. He looked at me in the rear-view mirror and asked yet another question about the fox. When I didn't reply, he started going on about Dad's big beard.

He had it all completely wrong. Dad's beard was clean and soft. Dad wasn't some crusty old hermit living in the mountains, he was just a dad, just the only one who hadn't made a big fuss about my cold hands thawed by the grey, still-warm throat, my cold hands stinking of death and the winter fox. He didn't even tell me off about my ruined gloves. He hugged me and comforted me, telling me about his own memories of childhood and foxes. Then we went to find the corpse, taking a pair of pliers to cut the snare, and we dug deep into the ground below the snow and buried it. He even cut off a hank of grey fur, which I added to the little treasure trove of memories I stored in the trunk of my tree and which, years later, helped me comfort my own children when they were upset. My dad knew just what to do, what to say and what not to say, everything the therapist would never understand.

# 9

# *Three Press-ups and Unable to Die*

It's not the first time. It's not my first time. As it's not the first time, people might think I failed. And talk about attempts. She made an attempt, they might say, with a look of distaste slightly tempered by compassion. But actually they can't, no one can say anything, no one's ever known or ever will, not even the kid who saved me.

They'll know about my death today, of course; I won't get it wrong again. They'll know about my death, but not that it was deliberate. I can't fail any more. Such a fluke couldn't happen twice, that would really be unlucky, and besides, so there's no risk at all, I've changed my route, I won't take the same road. I can't run that risk again, the risk of not dying, of not dying so others can live, as I did that first time. If I were to fail again, I wouldn't try any more. I'd force myself to live, to carry on – and that I simply can't do any more. I didn't actually fail the first time, I just made sure the kid didn't die. After that, there was no way I could have another go. It took me a while to pull myself together. I know it's hard to understand. The kid's play at dying shook me so badly I felt threatened; my decision to end my life was undermined. And with dying, if you no longer have to do it, then you can't do it: you can't choose to do it. Nothing must deflect you from your determination to die. Something tiny may revive you – for a time. An endless time. That kid and his crazy performance brought me back to life and I was in remission for a month. After a month, I came to my senses and got back in the car. I regained my certainty with relief.

I chose a car accident because they're easy to fake. Not to cause more suffering than necessary. I don't love my family enough to stay alive; just enough to lie to them one last time and protect them from their guilt. I don't want them to think they didn't love me enough, especially not my children. I am the one who doesn't feel anything. I feel nothing, almost nothing, and I can't say it, I can't live with it. Nothing for anyone, not even for myself, not even for my children. I feel nothing inside, and my outward existence suffocates me. I have to bear my own weight, the weight of my body, this armour, this shell that is me and is choking me.

I've had more than enough of myself, I must get rid of this self. I'm leaving me. Other people provide no refuge: they mass together instead of lightening my load, they lay their own armour upon my already overburdened carcass and their touch is heavy. Other people are an excess weight, my children especially. I can't do it any longer, can't carry anyone, anything more. Each encounter exhausts me, and with myself it's the worst. There: I can't bear myself any longer. Feeding myself, getting up, washing, sleeping, sleeping again. The sleeping part I can just about manage but the rest, no. Going out. Standing up, holding a book, opening my eyes. I can't do it any more. I simply can't.

I've tried for so long and so often to lighten the load of living, like when you're swimming. All I wanted was to float. I've tried to float. I've tried life, love, I've tried drinking and all sorts of drugs. I've tried motherhood too. But everything has been a burden. I tried so hard to swim through all that. Water pressure does resist atmospheric pressure – for a while. But then it's not enough and my body sinks again.

In the end, what's kept me alive for days and days in spite of everything is all the planning required to die. To die without seeming to try, all the organization to set up the accident. And then, after the kid, when I screwed up my death, I kept myself going with everything I imagined about his life and especially the landscape around him. It was a ritual, a daily exercise. Sometimes I made do with the colours. I pictured his world as an array of greys and blacks, from morning through to dusk. From his morning until his evening, greys and blacks – this at any point in my own days. I pictured pools behind his apartment block, pools extending haphazardly around water-treatment plants, and in these pools were swans, keeping a wary distance, handsome swans like a mistake, invaders rooting amid the wintry water for small holes the ice hadn't yet sealed off. I'm rarely mistaken about landscapes. I fill them in around people I meet. This is no fancy; I have good topographical instincts. I made the swans' feathers in the middle of that urchin's grey days grey like the rest, but such a pale grey they were almost white, a dirty white, pecked at by beaks that dazzled, being so out of place among those open tanks whose usually nauseating odour was made bearable by the cold. I know that only a few kilometres away, as the swan flies, you come to the glass-recycling plant where other birds rot from frostbite and forgetting. Not just birds, a great assortment of dead animals, domestic and farmyard, meant for consumption or as pets, bodies ignorantly thrown in with the broken glass. No one knows quite how to get rid of them, they think no one will see them in among the glass, no one will realize. More often in with the glass than the cardboard, Lord knows why. Filling in this landscape took up the time I had to live. I started with a suitable mist, brooding but not too dense, so you could still see and the scene was still quite ugly, and certainly not veiled by a fog that would have hazed everything into soft focus. I marched my young ragamuffin from side to side through the scene, looking a little stupid and very forlorn. He threw stones at the swans – of course. Those deeply cold days in the city, the frost enveloped objects and lightly fringed them with lace, but no one appreciated

the fineness of that grey, the frothy needlework, for we
didn't like the cold, we don't like it, when it freezes our
fingertips all the way up to our words, to our mouths,
when to speak is to fracture chapped lips and to walk is to
shake off a sulky numbness that we prefer to any outing,
any conversation. Strangely, this frostbitten, ambient sulk,
and the kid's constrained and filthy daily reality, forced
me to get up, they brightened my days. They kept me
going for a month like that, as my days with the children
used to do when they were around and young, when I was
busy being a mother, that everyday busyness, so absorb-
ing, which lifted me up, which lent me wings. When the
children needed me. Now they're grown up and my life
is shorn of the feathers of their dependence. Separated
from me, they've become a burden. My children have
flown and I can no longer muster a wingbeat.

Leading on to the motorway, the faulty sign warned of
'high wins'. I didn't know how to interpret this trun-
cated message, if indeed I should interpret it. I drove on
despite the high wins. The kid catapulted into the start of
my death like something lawless, the way a wind-blown
plastic bag violently plasters itself across a windscreen,
the way a blinded bird plummets at top speed, the way
an abandoned animal throws itself under your wheels,
with no ill intentions, with no intentions at all. He'd
given no thought to the accident he could have caused –
or rather he had, but with such disregard, such a pre-
adolescent irresponsibility, that everything else had paled

in comparison. Above all, he hadn't thought for a second, not before, after or even during the event, of the accident he'd prevented. In his game with death, this dare he must have imagined to be total, he'll never know he's been playing not with someone's life but with their death. He had not, as he'd believed, run the risk of an accident; instead he'd prevented the certainty of one – mine, the accident I had planned so meticulously.

There is no such thing as silence on the motorway. There are all the associated noises, the gears, engines, the hum of the other cars, air friction over metal, vibrations spinning off behind us, vacuumed up. The windscreen takes some of the pressure, but it reduces the roar of our journeys only by a fraction.

There were four or five of them, none older than twelve, emerging one at a time to play their game. This consisted of each boy running across the motorway and turbo-charging his terror by doing press-ups mid-carriageway, the number presumably announced in advance, with much pomp and strutting. The one I so nearly hit managed three before he sprang up.

I've done that, done what I could of it – press-ups, exercise, even dance – to escape my weight, my density, before I realized that this heaviness came not from my body but from my whole self. From within me. I did try to lift my heavy body in the gym. I went every evening, I believed in it, but I was scared too, scared of meeting people; I couldn't stand adding to my burden, augmenting it with the sediment of more people. I grew ugly so I'd be left in peace, it's so easy to do. Press-ups are easy too, raising your body on your fingertips. All that, I could do. But I found no liberation that way; dying is all I can do now to escape this clinging encrustation, this thick rot that is me. I'm not fat – it's not that; I'm not overweight: it's my whole life that's obese. Press-ups, sit-ups, the lot; I've tried everything to tame my body, its humours, its excitements, its losses. I thought taming my body would allow me to forget it. I did sit-ups until it burned, I ran till I could hardly breathe, I exercised anticipating the pain: I believed in its power to purge. I was mistaken. I thought I was dissolving my body in relatively affordable discomfort, but it grew all the more present. It vibrated. It resonated. It told tales on me. I felt like a blind person testing the ground ahead with my cane; holding on had become a prison, a film I still struggled to pierce, and my white cane was made of all my nerves bound together, a wad of nerves, entwined, fused, alive. All I wanted, all I want is to cut these bonds, to scatter and destroy them. To desensitize myself all over, from head to toe, to die, die, die. I stay in shape – that's what I used to say to those who were surprised to see me so regularly on the treadmill, but it was the opposite, of course: I wanted to undo myself, to destroy my shell. I had my body down for landfill.

When I was very young, I had a recurring nightmare. I'm not sure it was a nightmare; I think it was a kind of near-reality, a feeling of being unable to wake up. This nightmare followed me into adolescence and still grips me now and then. It was there before and there during each awakening. I couldn't get out of my sleeping body. I was spent. Waking up was exhausting. I had to muster vast amounts of energy to move even my little finger. I knew I was awake but I couldn't move, could hardly breathe. I was choking and desperate somehow to know if I was still asleep or had already woken. If I was already awake, why couldn't I move even the smallest part of me? And if still asleep, how was it I had this awareness of not being able to wake completely? I think I was in between, in a half-sleep or a half-waking. I even feel I'm still there, between sleeping and waking, between dying and living; I'm always there, I've always been there. When, in the end, with my last gasp and last ounce of energy, I managed to lift a finger, I would make one further effort, an extra, last effort, to look at the finger, to make sure it had moved, that it was moving, and what I'd see then was even more terrifying than the paralysis. I'd see a transparent finger, a false finger, pass over my true finger. My body was dividing in two. I'd scream out, I really would, I'd push the scream till it came out, expelled. I'd hold my breath and wake myself up completely. But not every time. Sometimes I stayed stuck in that scream and the scream stuck inside me. The difficulty of moving my body on waking up, the difficulty of waking up, was – though I was so young – a kind of morning melancholy, a difficulty with living which woke and rose before me. I was shifting parts of my body without moving, transparent limbs that weren't my own, copies of my limbs, false starts of myself.

I've always had a double: my doppelgänger was my cousin, we were like twins, so alike that we used to play 'drunken mirrors' together, creating multiple reflections of our profiles in the bathroom mirrors. We were identical, truly, but she was wild and full of life. I thought I'd spotted her at my daughter's wedding some years ago. I was shocked to see her so weak, so ill and sad; she looked nothing like me now, except that she was so sad and tired. Actually it was a mistake, someone with the same name. I'd lost touch with my real cousin, I'd lost her, she who'd been so alive, who so resembled me, like a living me, me but alive. She left home and hit the road very early, barely eighteen, hungry to discover what she called 'elsewhere'. I had no desire to see how life goes on elsewhere; waking up really was too painful and my life-weariness so advanced. It was a total fatigue that ground away my body, skin first, then eroded my flesh, all the way down to my bones and nerves, a fatigue long beyond my control.

I haven't seen my cousin again in all this time, since she left home for elsewhere.

The kid was in a tracksuit and his arrogant eyes saw nothing but the cars speeding past. He of course had no idea that we couldn't see his gaze and appreciated nothing of his feat, neither I nor the other drivers. Everything happened so slowly for me, without fear and without adrenalin, that I pitied their motorway romantics. I remember how the seconds slowed; it seems this is often the way with accidents. I remember my reflexes' instant, calm response, and my fury at having fucked up my attempt. In my red fog at being unable to die, I spun a full 180 degrees and found myself facing backwards on the hard shoulder. I saw my movements separately one by one, my thoughts emerging in order, my own life in slow motion as I saved the kid's.

Where had this little shit come from? He wasn't from any world I knew. He was from beyond the road, from a parallel world, the one that begins over the verge, after the hard shoulder, he came from behind the crash barrier. I'd never strayed into this region before, never ventured as far as these motorway sub-roads, these ditches. It seems the end of the world is everywhere we experience isolation, divergence without signposts. I who like to control everything, I who control nothing, I didn't even think about this, didn't even consider it, right up until he did his defiant aerobics in front of me, that kid, bringing my clear-eyed journey towards death to a violent halt. He'd just deflected me from suicide. I was alive and diverted. I looked around and then up: there was movement above, in my rear-view mirror. His friends were there, on the bridge where the A-road crossed the motorway. They were lined up along that other road as if at the theatre, filming us on their phones and swearing futilely at the roaring void, in an idiotic state of excitement, made even more pathetic by their high-tech accessories.

I set off again amid extraordinary silence: there had been no one, no slowing down, no curiosity, in those few long seconds. I no longer wanted to die; I blamed myself, blamed the kid. I didn't want to die then for more than a month, took all that time to return to my senses, to return to dying. Dazed and angry. In avoiding the accident, that desire for death seemed to have evaporated, my death plan was shattered. I came back to my life little by little, doing things one at a time; it took me a while. A month and here I am, back again. A new shell, a new version of myself has come together, as constricted as the one before. It's my cage, I choke on life. I must be rid of myself. I can't – I can no longer – do anything else. You must understand: I've neither enough fear nor enough light-heartedness to live.

I'm not taking the motorway this time.

And him, right there, it can't be true, I didn't see him. He must've been in my blind spot. He's hitchhiking, I don't believe it, he's stopped me, now he's here, right in front of the car, this can't happen again, it's beyond belief, all over again, their love of life and of playing with it. With fear.

# 10

## *Over the Aqueduct*

All of us who live near the new port know the aqueduct. The towpaths that stretch either side of the water have shaped our bored Sundays for donkeys' years, doubtless since the aqueduct was built. Patrick and I spent years traipsing along them with our parents, from one end to the other, there and back and back again. When we'd grown out of holding our mothers' hands we still went to the aqueduct, but then we used to go hiding inside it, in the middle level where the railway ran between the arches. We would listen to the two waters. The water above us, the canal water, regularly pulsed downward, towards us, by the barges and pleasure boats, water ringing with the sounds of navigation and the distorted conversations of passers-by; and the water below, the river water, often in spate, weightier and wilder too, but without other noise than its own, its own currents, the mass of it beating against its banks. We used to flatten ourselves against the arches when goods trains went by; there weren't many and we had their timetables by heart. All those odd and conflicting noises intrigued us. We liked trying to guess which boats were below us, which above; and from below we would savour glimpses of those strolling on the towpaths, Sunday visitors among whom we proudly no longer counted ourselves. The bikes, the little kids, the old biddies and the girls of course, mostly walking in pairs or threes. We were a pair: Pat and me. We were best friends in the whole world, as they say, in every possible world I think, actually. Proud of being older, of operating secretly, proud of being together. And so impatient: impatient to grow up, to grow up some more, impatient to see things happen. Round here, both above and below, so little happened, so slowly, the world stood still right along the canal, and if something did push ahead, it was at barge-speed, just ten kilometres an hour. Even the goods trains dawdled. Together we dreamed of supersonic speed, of escape.

From our secret HQ, if one of us held on to the other and we found the right angle, we could look straight up girls' skirts. We were more fascinated than excited. We never managed to match particular thighs to particular girls, but we loved to lose ourselves in speculation. Imagining was enough. To know for sure, one of us would have had to go up on to the aqueduct and stroll on the towpath with one eye on his watch, while the other kept guard alone below and noted the precise time so as to ascertain who was wearing blue knickers (for example), to tally up the minutes and seconds and the secret stares. For we knew all the girls round about, even the summer visitors. We thought of the system with the watches much too late. We only ever managed to pin one name to one bottom. And later, after what happened, we didn't want to play there any more.

That one bottom obsessed us more than the others. It was no longer enough to guess; we had to know. Why, I can hardly say. The girl's backside was no lovelier than any other, her underwear was ordinary, old-fashioned even, but we were drawn to her, no question. First, she didn't walk like the others: she had a very slight limp, like a hesitation, a stuttering step, the gait of a little child. Occasionally she would stumble. Also, she carried on strange conversations with another woman, an old lady, probably her mother or grandmother. After spying obsessively for several days, one morning we were caught out and narrowly avoided a dousing of dirty water tossed into the river from the aqueduct. Very dirty even: stinking, with piss and the rest of it in there too, I think. We quickly realized, or quickly decided rather, that the old lady had spotted us and rewarded us with the contents of a chamber pot for our caddish behaviour. But it was the 1980s, people had stopped using chamber pots like that a good while back. Words like that too: cad. And yet that's what she – what the mother – was to pin on us: that word, though not yet. We're not quite at that point in my story. My grandmother had told me about chamber pots, how people used to go to the toilet in the old days, but we were no longer in the old days. No need to check our watches, all at once we knew who they were. There were only two women as backward as these in the village. We made enquiries and yes, as outdated and squalid as it may seem, they did indeed use chamber pots and empty them from the aqueduct. Like in the old days.

That put us right off our game. Straight away, we began to cast around for a new one. Still hidden inside the aqueduct, under the arches. Talking about it now makes me ashamed all over again and I think, more than life, more than time, that was what came between us, between Pat and me. Yet we truly used to be best friends in the world, and our absolute confidence as a pair carried us a long way between those two watercourses. Perhaps too far.

The younger one, the daughter, wasn't that young but well into her twenties above her girlish legs, a good ten or fifteen years older than us, and we knew she was a virgin, as pure as she was simple. As for her mother, who must have been nearly sixty, she handled her daughter, a slow, retarded child, the old-fashioned way. Her mother was holding her back even more, as if her disability, her isolation and backwardness, weren't enough. They dressed, or rather the mother dressed the pair of them, like my grandmother, like the old people in the village, and that gave the daughter's body an odd shape, a shape that wasn't in the least attractive, and yet. And yet now we couldn't leave them alone. All our conversations came back to the two backward women, and all those conversations finished back in the same place, every time: crouched in the aqueduct's middle level, we returned over and over to the virginity problem. It bothered us, to say the least. We mocked, but we were also curiously upset, even moved by it. Of course we didn't say as much; between ourselves we admitted only to the mockery, to the dumb jokes of that teenage time and the sniggering. We wanted to do something about her. We spent weeks puzzling over the origins and future of the madwomen, the mother's past, who the father might be and the daughter's future: her future, her man, her husband. Was it possible there could even be one, one day? Even for a day? One single man? We weren't men. We weren't smart enough to teach her the facts of life, not bold enough to bed her, not cruel enough to force her and not sufficiently attracted to seduce her.

We had to find someone else. What we both had, Pat and I, more than anyone else, was wild imaginations, and these went completely rampant when we were together, in our little eyrie between the two waters.

We no longer looked on from below but from above. We watched the river down below. Sometimes we would hear, smell and see the arc of the chamber pot, and we'd be secretly in stitches. One day, blown off course by the wind, its contents misfired over the riverbank. Near that bank there was a coach stop, the one for the city. We had a fit of giggles just thinking that the pot's contents could have ended up on the windscreen. The goods train went by, drowning out our laughter, and it was then that we had our idea. We don't have passenger trains in our small town any more; journeys to other places are all done by coach. It was at the coach stop below, under the aqueduct, that we would marry off our protégée.

Today I've got to take that coach again, for the first time in I don't know how long. My wife needs the car and I couldn't tell her why I didn't want to take the coach.

We went up before going down; we went up to tell them. One damp and chilly Friday they were alone on the aqueduct, walking arm in arm, like in the old days. We used our politest formulae to approach them. Mistrustful at first, the mother ended by hearing us out. We spoke only to her but our subject was her daughter. We had just returned from the city, where we'd had a meeting with the doctor, the specialist, the one from the highly respected surgery on the boulevard. He was so pleasant that we'd easily and naturally fallen into conversation, and when he learned that we were from here, he'd talked straight away about the young lady he had seen on the aqueduct. We explained to the mother that we'd been unable to refrain from informing him about the said young lady, though that may have been somewhat presumptuous, we conceded. The doctor from the city! Hardly forty and so elegant; perhaps they knew him by sight? No, they didn't know him, but the mother was hooked. The daughter seemed not to understand and the mother punished her for this with a discreet little slap. We were too deep in our game to appreciate the implication of that blow. For several Sundays, then, we acted as go-betweens from the city to the mother, between doctor and daughter, via the mother, on the aqueduct over the river. The mother stopped emptying their chamber pot into it. One day we brought a more important message. We pointed out the coach stop and explained that one Saturday, when the surgery usually closed, the doctor would come to enquire for her hand. We chose outdated words that we barely knew how to use, and were also barely able to keep from laughing, laughter that we at last let rip back in our middle level, as soon as we'd made it down there.

And it was there that we settled, behind an arch, every Saturday after that. They would arrive in time for the first coach, then they'd be back for the afternoon coach and lastly for the evening one, all dressed up, every Saturday. The daughter would be wearing a forced smile, a dogged grimace that we began to find worrying. After a few months during which their clothes hardly varied with the seasons, we noticed a new shawl round the daughter's neck. The mother was on edge and kept telling her to make an effort, to make herself presentable. Her words rose up to us, now amplified by the bridge's echo, now muffled by the noise of the waters above and below. Exasperated by the girl's indifference to yet another non-appearance by the doctor, the mother gave the shawl a tug. The daughter's cry reached us just before the goods train came through. The train went by, the coach moved off again, we looked at each other and we talked. We decided to stop the joke, it had to stop now. And only we could stop it.

We were not quite as polite in our confession, one Saturday after the last coach from the city had gone, and that may be why the mother called us cads. We'd meant nothing caddish in playing that joke; I don't know how the mother reached that conclusion, with her twisted mind, simple but twisted, but this time she did not believe us. We were cads to claim it had been a joke; the doctor must have so much work to do, he would come when he could, who were we to know better than her, he would come and that was the end of it. We'd made up this story of a joke out of jealousy, caddishness and jealousy, that was all. The daughter seemed to be disappearing into her shawl, which she'd now tied right around her head; she wore no particular expression and her little girl's skip came back, there on the riverbank, at the coach stop beneath the aqueduct, when the two of them turned back again.

All of us who live near the new port know the aqueduct. Every Saturday, the towpaths that stretch either side of the water are full of local people taking the air. For years now, they've watched the pair of madwomen heading towards the intercity coach stop. Their comments are always the same: somewhere between mockery and sympathy. The coach drivers know the story, as do all the villagers, and they always have a kind word for the women now, having, like many others, given up trying to reason with them. It was only a childish joke. No one ever knew exactly who set it up. The mother persists, the daughter goes along, she's grown old in her shawl. I don't know what has become of Pat. They say that the daughter had a suitor, once, a drifting, grief-stricken widower, but the mother saw to it that the daughter made no promises but kept herself for the doctor. I don't like to guess how the mother wielded such control over her, for so long and even now.

I can feel a lump in my throat at the sigh of the closing doors but I'm slightly comforted by the driver's unvarying words to the women: next Saturday perhaps, right, then, good evening to you. I take a seat on the coach for the first time in many years. The shawl has lost all colour, the mother too is ageless now, she smiles at me through the window, next Saturday, yes, of course, right.

# 11

## *The Mini-pilgrimage*

I braked hard because of a hitchhiker. I didn't see him until he loomed up in my rear-view mirror like an apparition, as though he was standing in a blind spot. A sort of phantom, a White Lady, a chimera, I don't know, but he was suddenly there and I slammed on the brakes. I could, I should have been afraid, but at the very moment when I should have panicked, something else happened that completely distracted me. Something that completely overturned my judgement, my fear, everything. When I braked, a pile of snow slipped off the roof of my car. Snow. In the middle of summer, and I hadn't even come from the mountains. A big lump of snow that had hardened on the roof and been sitting there for I don't know how long. I walked around my car, and the man, the phantom hitchhiker, did the same in the opposite direction. We bumped into each other and then, well, there I was at a standstill, stunned, so I thought I might as well pick him up. Things weren't settled in my life. I never normally pick up hitchhikers, but that day it had snowed, in midsummer, on my car. No, things weren't settled. When the snow fell down, or actually just before it fell from the roof of my car, just before I braked because of the hitchhiker, I was thinking about my wife, her brother and her mother. It was such an involved story that even thinking about it was already complicated. You couldn't think about it just like that, idly. You had to do something with your hands or your legs, make your body do some kind of repetitive activity to guide the unfolding of all those family relationships, and try to see clearly in that overflowing cave that was my wife's family, tidy up a bit of the mess in there, try to breathe. Driving was better than doing nothing; it helped me to think about that story, but it wasn't enough. I needed to walk, do some gardening or housework or ironing, go to the gym, do press-ups.

If it snows in the middle of summer, I thought to myself, it's like a miracle. I didn't believe in the supernatural, I didn't believe in God and what have you, and I definitely didn't believe in men, not any more. I thought all those things to myself, but out loud I just talked about the snow, trying to appreciate the whole absurdity of it. The whole way I bored the poor bloke I'd picked up with the story of the miraculous snow, but all the while I didn't stop thinking about my wife's situation, about how to save her, help her find her way out of that vault, the family vault where she'd just buried her mother and where she'd ended up finding, digging up, her older brother. Wrong in the head, he'd been hidden from the world by her mother. Or actually he hadn't, not exactly, because the story was really, really complicated and intricate and impossible to untangle. My wife knew him but she didn't know he was her brother. Through shame or some kind of perversion of motherly love – total love, or perhaps incomplete, unsatisfied love – her mother had always pretended her son was her domestic help, her handyman. Throughout her childhood my wife had lived with this man, who was already grown up when she was born because she was a late child, and she lived alongside him never knowing he was her brother. I knew him well because we saw him often. He looked after our son just as he'd looked after my wife when she was a little girl. Our son is an adult now, and this man, my brother-in-law, is an old man, an old man with a child's mind. I was lost in my questions, those unsettled questions, in worry about my wife, and then there was the snow. Snow. And I kept wondering aloud about it, this snow, and couldn't stop talking about it to the hitchhiker, who was clearly bored. He didn't seem as surprised as I was by this snow on my bonnet; he probably thought I was a bit crazy and that I'd really come from a place, who knows where, some kind of place where snow falls in summer, some kind of isolated plateau, but I wasn't admitting to it, or I'd forgotten about it, or something. Because places like that exist in this country, I know they do, they're like other countries inside our own, with summer snow, and we'd already been to a special place like that, my wife, my son and I. We'd rented a gîte and, yes, we'd touched

July snowflakes. It was a place where there were strange stories going around, unsavoury ones, legends of foxes killing themselves, of a little girl made into fertilizer for pumpkins, all quite hard to believe and told by a mad old man they called the automatic tour guide whose mouth would open as soon as you passed the door of his hut. But I hadn't brought back any snow that summer, it hadn't snowed enough to cover the car, not even enough to walk through. I hadn't crunched through snow since I was twelve years old. My hitchhiker wanted to tell his own story about how he knew some mad people too, more like roadside loonies, but I didn't let him get a word in edgeways. All I wanted to do was talk about snow, chew snow with each word I said. I was obviously getting on his nerves, going on and on about impossible snowflakes, my sentences burying him in this snow that had in fact disappeared with the heat and speed and now didn't exist except in my mouth. Actually I was thinking about something else; with all this snow in my mouth, I wasn't even thinking about my wife's brother but about my own childhood, my own family. About the last time in my life it had snowed, my last tracks in the snow.

The last time I saw snow close up, enough to leave tracks in it, the last time I walked through snow, was also the first time I think, perhaps the only time in my life, I'm not sure, but it's my clearest memory of snow.

Two or three weeks before Christmas, all those years ago, it had snowed at the Bonne Mère, the great Notre-Dame-de-la-Garde basilica. It had snowed over the whole city, but the only place where it stayed until morning was the Bonne Mère, by the old Joan of Arc tank, the starting point for our mini-pilgrimage. My mother was very devout and the whole family would go on mini-pilgrimages. She also did a whole lot of God things by herself: Bible study groups and paths of initiation into praying the psalms. Because, she would say, the psalms are part of the Eucharist celebration, which isn't just for priests or monks or nuns but for us all. For us all. She would open her arms to hold us all, or the three of us at least, her, Dad and me. Also, she said, making an exaggerated mime of grasping a handle and going in somewhere, it's a good way into the Old Testament. The psalms are the echo, in prayer, of the lived history of Israel's followers and all God's people. She would clasp her hands, her eyes shining, and sometimes she wrapped her arms around herself in a corny self-hug. They are where the Christian story gains its true meaning, she said, pressing her hands together hard, her fingers like talons, the knuckles whitening. They are where our own history as believers in Jesus Christ still finds words for prayer. I was fascinated by the lyricism of her idiocy and her emphatic gestures, so fascinated and disheartened that I still know her pronouncements and her gestures by heart, those mad pronouncements about God's love, those ridiculous gestures as she talked to me about cries of distress, protestations against evil, praise and thanks for our Lord's acts of salvation, hope for us all beyond our earthly selves, the joy of seeing the dawn of a new

world of justice and peace, hymns to the God of creation and history . . . She would often go to discussion
groups to talk about these things and afterwards, in the
evening, she'd read me the psalm in question. They were
beautiful, I must admit, like poems. But our life wasn't
any better for them, it wasn't better than other people's.
The meaning of our life remained invisible and it was
still nowhere in sight when I found myself, on the brink
of adolescence, at the start of what was to be my last
mini-pilgrimage, one snowy Saturday in Marseilles at
ten in the morning. I was twelve.

I was sick of mini-pilgrimages, especially in winter
when the mistral was in full swing. Our meeting point
was Joan's tank and that day there was snow. Not much,
but it was slippery and sly, concealing ice on the sloping
paths that threatened to embellish my boredom with
some memorable pratfalls, but I wasn't in the mood to
laugh. And of course there were the grannies. To please
Mum, we had to look after the grannies. These pilgrim-
ages were a new sort, intergenerational. It was so that
young and old could come together to walk and reflect,
to exchange ideas, but actually the young people served as
talking walking sticks for the old. Lean on me, Madame,
I'll help you, I'm here to help, you know, yes, to listen as
well. I longed for the moments of prayer, when I could
escape the endless complaints and repetitions of these
bigoted women from Marseilles who'd lost the use of
everything except their tongues. I didn't like touching
old people, or anybody. I hated the moment in the Mass

when we had to hold hands and kiss each other. I hated human warmth.

Quarter past ten, informal discussion by Joan's tank, and each participant was given a sheet so they could reflect on the texts and sing. With the old lady I'd been given that day there was no chance of reflection, but there was no shortage of singing, completely out of tune and toothless. Half past ten, ascent and prayer, and I had to support her, the snow escaping from under her feet so that with each step her shoes, almost slippers, touched the ice that had barely melted even with the salt, her whole body seeming to absorb each shock as she tottered along, and me, only twelve years old, forty kilos, about the same as her, and Mum, Mum, I could feel her right behind me, looking at me, proud and seeking forgiveness. She was so devout, Mum, that I couldn't help thinking she must have done something that needed forgiving. Eventually we'd reach the crypt, where we would celebrate the receiving of the light just before lunch. The higher we got, the larger and more useless the lumps of salt were, so the snow had hardened like concrete on its layer of ice, but I stuck at it, I held on to my old pilgrim of the day. I bottled up all my disgust, my desire to abandon it all, my first little revolts against the whole world, and especially against Mum's world, the snowy, Catholic, Marseilles world.

I sat down near my little old lady, who was skinny and freezing, worn out by this tiny pilgrimage, and I watched her watching the speaker, the priest, with her mouth open as though she'd never heard anyone speak before, her mouth open and her breath stale, as though she'd lacked air and water all her life. Watching her made me feel ill and I suddenly understood who this old woman was. This dried-up, forgotten shadow was Mum, it was what Mum would become. So I knew this was the last time. I breathed in the breath of this old woman right there in the crypt and suddenly I got up. I couldn't follow Mum ever again on mini-pilgrimages, or in any of her little obsessions, her dubious activities. I became one of those countless teenage idiots who turn against everything all at once and there was nothing Mum could do. It was easy to be twelve years old, to say no and not see Mum grow old.

I stopped when my passenger asked me to. He pointed out that all the snow had gone but rain was moving in from the west. I didn't have any stories about rain to think about. He got out and said thanks, hope you make it all right. How can I make it all right?

# 12

# *The Dropout*

I recognized you straight away, even from behind, from the way you walk: it makes you look slightly unbalanced or ruffled. You don't limp, exactly, or really look annoyed, just folded, a bit wonky. I stopped. You turned round and I saw your name badge before I even looked at your face. It was you, no doubt about it. You were folding away your face as though you wanted to hide it. You got in the car without resisting, but then why would you have resisted? You were hitchhiking, I stopped and you were very confused, not even recognizing me. Why would you have resisted? You didn't look at me and you were trying to hide your wrinkled, troubled, trembling face, so how could you have recognized me?

You got in, fastened your seat belt and, very gingerly, as though it hurt to do so, unfolded yourself. You drew your face out of your body and looked at me. You stared right at me and I could see in your eyes that my face reminded you of something, but what? You couldn't place me; you saw me without recognizing me. You'd seen my face somewhere and here it was now in front of you, in front of you and elsewhere in an elusive memory, my recognized but unrecognized face, my face on the tip of your tongue. You smiled as if to thank me.

It was you, first of all; it was you we didn't recognize. Not just then, in the evening by the side of the road, hitchhiking, but earlier, all afternoon at the wedding. Even I didn't recognize you. How could I have recognized you? You looked so unlike me, and yet we used to look so alike. Well no, not you, my cousin, my cousin and I were so alike. She and I were like almost-twins, offbeat twins. My cousin is a bit younger than me, but only by a few days, and a bit shorter too.

I remember a game we played as children, a game just for us that only we could play, my cousin and I. We would carefully set up mirrors in just the right place in the bathroom so that we could see only our profiles in them. My cousin's face would be just below mine like a repetition – not really a reflection, more of a stuttering image. Her face, the same, my face, just below itself, repeated, doubled. We called the game 'drunken mirrors'.

There was no way I could have recognized you because you weren't her, clearly. Despite your badge with her name on it, my cousin's name, you weren't her. Nobody understood, not even me. We understood that you weren't her but we didn't understand what you were doing there or who you were. We didn't try to understand. My cousin hadn't turned up, maybe because of some kind of delay, and you were there, wearing her name on a badge. My cousin didn't play by the rules: if you're delayed, you warn people, and if you're not coming, you don't just drop out, you cancel. A few people always cancel before a wedding, even right at the last minute. It's very annoying but you cope, you juggle the seating plan, move people around, put them on different tables, make sure men and women are evenly distributed. It's very rude to drop out, and just as rude not to warn anyone of a delay. We were wondering whether my cousin might have had an accident when you began to draw attention to yourself. At first, this distracted us from our worrying, but then it threw us into a state of embarrassment that was much worse. We all thought, blinded as we are by our prejudices, that it was some kind of joke in poor taste, then we thought you must be a gatecrasher. Otherwise, why wear the badge? This tramp had stolen our name to eat, drink and party at our expense. Especially drink, we whispered among ourselves, because your ruined face was unmistakably that of an alcoholic. You'd seen the surname on a badge, my maiden name and my cousin's too, and you'd chosen a first name at random, which happened to be my cousin's. It's a common first name. Still – and now I know, it seems so easy to understand; now I remember noticing straight away and rejecting the thought just as quickly – you didn't drink a drop of alcohol, and with good reason.

*

Why wear that great big badge? That was the first thing I asked when you got into my car, just after your thanks and your long stare, and before I even tried to find out where you were going. Why the badge? You replied in one long exhalation, so long that you almost seemed breathless, or unwilling to get your breath back, unwilling to stop talking. You replied in one long surge of words, your mouth trembling so I had trouble understanding you. You told, trembled, breathed the whole story of being ill and needing daily care.

You need to go back to the diabetes clinic, where a nurse is expecting you for your dialysis tomorrow morning. You're lost. You didn't know, you still don't know, how to manage all this. The clinic had sorted out your train journey but you'd had to leave much earlier than expected because in the end, actually, you weren't invited to the wedding, so you didn't know what to do or how to get back to the station by bus, with all that time to wait and then the bus and the train. And you couldn't take an earlier train because the ticket can't be refunded or exchanged, or something like that, you don't know about that sort of thing, you go out so little, hardly ever. So you had the idea of hitchhiking but you weren't sure if the clinic allowed that. In fact you hadn't really thought it through. You'd left on a sudden impulse, or because you were angry, you can't really remember, it was before, it was now, and it wasn't such a good idea because, having left earlier, you were actually going to be late, you might even miss the train, the one you had to get in the evening, the one you were supposed to take in the first place, and you'd miss your dialysis in the morning, and if I could, oh, if I could take you to the station and lend you the money for the ticket, so as to get an earlier train, and not miss the evening one, or help you to change your ticket, it would really set your mind at rest. All I'd have to do would be to give you my address and the clinic would reimburse me, they're so nice, without them goodness knows . . .

You'd stopped looking at me again. You were muddling up the timetables and the journeys, completely disorientated. You'd retracted your face into your body again. I promised to do all that, yes of course, absolutely. And then, only then, you breathed again, and you turned your face towards me. That face that we all, myself included, recognized immediately as that of an alcoholic, a face irrevocably marked and lined by drink, the skin puffy and criss-crossed by little burst blood vessels, greasy and covered in pimples, tiny beginnings of some kind of infection, and those pale eyes, red and faded, prematurely old. With those eyes you looked at me. You looked at me for so long I was afraid you'd recognize me, but it was an absent look, and from that absence tears sprang. You were crying hard now, crying with as much energy as you had put into trying to explain yourself a minute ago, but without words now, without anger. Your face is finally comprehensible, justified by the tears, its red, swollen skin explained by the crying. You smiled at me and I realized that you still hadn't recognized me, perhaps because of the tears. You thanked me as you blew your nose clumsily with the tissue I'd just given you. I'm not completely sure it was a thank you but it was something like it, mixed up with an inelegant snort from your nose and mouth. Nothing you do is elegant, it must be said, and perhaps that was what made my daughter so very angry. Mother, look what she's wearing, she kept saying, and I said, What about you, darling, look at the state you're getting yourself into. It's not so bad, pull yourself together. You took another deep breath, one more long breath, without trembling this time, and you said how kind I was, just like the people at the clinic, not like the bride.

When you said that word I jumped, realizing that in my haste I hadn't taken the decorations off the car and, as though I'd spoken my thoughts aloud, as though you'd understood why I'd jumped, you smiled very discreetly, perhaps just to yourself, and asked me if, like you, I was on my way to or from a wedding. You looked embarrassed and said how beautifully dressed I was, but you just didn't have the money. I replied that my daughter was getting married. So it was a very important day. You seemed reassured, saying that of course, if I was The Family. You didn't say 'family' or 'one of the family' but 'The Family', stressing the words, but what about you, what were you if you weren't The Family? You seemed reassured, as though my close relationship to the bride justified my get-up much more convincingly than social conventions, wealth, status or obvious spending power. Anyway, those people, the ones at the wedding you'd been to, or rather that you hadn't been to, because they'd been so unbelievably rude, they may have been well dressed, like me (you said 'like you' with a little knowing look, as though you'd finally recognized me, but now I think about it, you can't have), they may have been well dressed but they didn't behave accordingly. You detached the word 'accordingly' as though touching it with only the tips of your fingers, the tip of your tongue, so as not to dirty yourself with it. There was no point dressing so nicely if they were only going to behave so coarsely. You had an invitation, you could show me if I didn't believe you, you'd been invited to this wedding. You were angry again. I believed what you were saying.

I couldn't believe it.

I had written the rough copy of that invitation myself, spending more time on it than on the others. I'd had to search for your address, and after several hours online I finally found some kind of PO box address. My cousin has always been what people describe as eccentric and I wasn't surprised by your address. I never imagined there'd be someone else with the same surname, because ours isn't very common. It's a surname we always thought of as prestigious and rare. An aristocratic name.

You calmed down a bit and apologized for the inconvenience. You might be making me miss my daughter's wedding, and that would be so bad, or perhaps you said look so bad, I couldn't hear very well. You began to realize all of a sudden and you wanted me to let you out and leave you at the roadside. By the side of this big road. 'That's out of the question,' I retorted, and I said it as a way of ending the conversation. That wasn't what I wanted. I wanted to ask you more and more things, but I didn't want to say too much about me and my presence here, on this road, all dressed up for a wedding. I wanted to know more and more, I wanted to ask questions, so many questions, but I didn't want to answer yours.

What I want to know most of all is who you are. Tell me, who are you if you're not my cousin?

I'll still have my doubts, you know, when I look at the wedding photos in a few days. It was when we were having the photos taken in front of the church that your behaviour started to arouse suspicion. You wanted to have your photo taken with the bride and groom and of course they refused. You thought it was a joke so you kept trying to squeeze into the side of the picture. I think you managed it a few times. I'll look at them and wonder if you were actually my cousin, if she'd changed, if you were her, if you'd ended up looking not like me any more. If she'd fallen ill. But no, she'd have told me, she'd have called out to me and laughed: don't you recognize me? She'd have laughed instead of insisting, as you did, that you were invited, that we couldn't just throw you out like that. Instead of shouting without being able to show that you had any link with the bride and groom. Because that's the question we asked, to get rid of our intruder: we asked if you were related to one of them. Or perhaps you really were my cousin but you'd lost your mind and your memory. You'd lost your memory and looked at us uncomprehendingly, unable to answer that question except by showing your invitation, my invitation, the invitation I worked on for so long, the invitation I sent you, clutched in your hand like a permit. And we pushed you away, we gave your invitation back to you. It must be a mistake, Madame, don't you see?

You didn't see. You made a scene, as my daughter said. She didn't want this tramp ruining her wedding, this madwoman making a scene, and I was so ashamed that I hung back, not daring to do anything one way or the other. I watched from a distance. I was ashamed of my daughter's behaviour and yours, and I was ashamed of our mistake, my mistake, because I was beginning to understand. I was too far away to read the address on the envelope but I understood, yes, I suddenly understood. I hung back and that's why you didn't recognize me when you got into the car.

My only movement, my only impulse, my only decision was to leave, afterwards. I left the wedding after the drinks; I left my own daughter's wedding and went off just like that. Just like that, those were the words in the text I got a few minutes ago, followed by a question mark. My daughter can be so rude when she loses the plot, despite being very prim most of the time. I left, just like that, without telling anyone, as they were going off to the venue where the grand meal for my daughter's grand wedding was happening, is actually happening at this very moment. I didn't follow the rest of the cars. I took the other road to try and find my cousin who isn't my cousin, and now here we are, the two of us, in my car, my non-cousin and me. You and me.

I look at you and I can't believe what I've done: abandoned my daughter on her wedding day. I abandoned her for you, you who are nothing to me, you who aren't one of the family, you whom I met, nonetheless, at my daughter's wedding, you who weren't invited, who were only invited because I made a mistake. My mistake invited itself, and you became guilty of accidental identity theft, I made you guilty of this theft. I'm still angry with you, though. You could have understood, or guessed. You didn't know those people, so why would they have invited you to their wedding? Why did you accept the invitation? You should have turned it down. If you'd thought about it for two minutes you wouldn't have got yourself into this mess, and you wouldn't have got us into this mess, the pair of us. I resent you, you know, but here I am, and I'll take you back to the station. I'll make sure you get back to the clinic and I'll return, unwillingly, to the festivities. To avoid any questions I'll say my cousin dropped out at the last minute.

I've still got that quiet, slick music in my head, the background music for the pre-dinner drinks. I'm surrounded by the murmurings of the CD, but is it that music, the background music at my daughter's wedding, or the memory of some other music, perhaps a music that was all yours, a musical noise coming from you? It was you

I was looking at during the drinks. I was watching you struggle. They'd taken you to one side and I didn't say anything, just blended into the background music. I stood there, seeing the contrast between the unobtrusive music and your anger, the distance between the utter discretion of that soft music and your coarseness as you argued, wanting to stay with us and come to the meal. The music in my head is your stubbornness. Now you're beating a rhythm on your leg with your finger, and I think you're beating time to some unfamiliar music, unfamiliar like you, music that comes from you, an inner musical murmur. This murmur, this music, comes out of you only through the ends of your fingers.

You kept asking questions during the drinks, like an uninhibited child brimming over with curiosity, wanting to know more than was seemly. You didn't fit with the tone of our unspoken codes of behaviour, our gentility, or even with the tone of the background music so carefully chosen by my daughter, that bland music where we took refuge. You changed the atmosphere with your questions; you broke the rhythm. I think it was your interruption of the rhythm that made us really see you as an intruder. You were dribbling a bit, as well. You couldn't hold your tongue. You asked so many questions and you couldn't keep it in your mouth, that tongue, even when you stopped talking. It kept coming out in an involuntary movement. There was always a little saliva around your mouth. It was embarrassing. If only you knew how embarrassing it was. But you did know, surely you knew.

You must have realized that there was a sudden empty space around you, and uneasy looks. You must have seen how out of place you were. Your questions, punctuated by that tic with your tongue, were so obtrusive that a waiter forced you to take some food, to shut you up. He needn't have bothered because you carried on opening your mouth, forgetting even the most basic good manners. You asked your questions with your mouth full, picking up the bits of food that your words forced out of your mouth with quick little flicks of your tongue. What other world do you belong to? Don't you even know that no one really talks at weddings? We just occupy the space, fill the silence. Language has no other function at a wedding, and the same goes for all sorts of other ceremonies. Talking is something that occupies our mouths, like canapés, to keep them away from real words and real questions.

My daughter stared at me in disgust and annoyance. She was commanding me, with that look, to get rid of you. You besieged us with questions but wouldn't answer ours. It even seemed as though you couldn't answer them, although they were simple. Who are you? Who invited you? Are you from the bride's family or the groom's? Now, in the car, you answer me in fits and starts. I have to choose my questions carefully so as not to arouse your suspicions. You mustn't realize what has happened, you mustn't understand why I'm here, why I picked you up even though my own daughter is celebrating her wedding at the end of a different road. You mustn't piece all the information together. You answer me in bursts, as though the answers come from within your body. You answer your own questions, which aren't really questions but just your panic. You try to make sense of the story. Why those people invited you and why they kicked you out.

You ask me what I think. You didn't know how to react or how to defend yourself. You don't know that there is no better weapon than approval, no better defence than saying yes. You said no endlessly, disrespectfully, in a high, forced voice. You brandished your indignant no, trying to slip it in between our sentences like a bad-mannered little girl weaving between the grown-ups' legs. You retreated into your no as you would into a corner. Beside yourself and surrounded. While everyone was setting off to the dinner venue, you kept asking who was going to give you a lift. When you realized there was nothing for it, they were refusing to listen to you, you couldn't force anyone to listen or to give you a lift, you just went off along the road, helpless as a child.

You ran away.

I was busy giving directions, organizing my little crowd, and I didn't see you escape. All the cars left the car park except mine and I was preparing to go and talk to you, to explain my mistake and apologize for us all, but you weren't there. I was worried, and I got in the car and drove off looking for you. As I searched, I kept going back over the business from the start, from the beginning of the misunderstanding. I wondered at what moment I could have cleared up the misunderstanding, prevented the damage or averted the accident. Now it's too late. You're an accident for me, you know, but life, if only you knew, but surely you do know, better than I do, life is just that, a whole lot of hitches, contradictions, mishaps and revisions, and it's all the better for that. It's the opposite of inertia. You're the opposite of inertia. You're the thing that contradicts, that makes us stumble. You're my hitchhiking tripwire.

We're almost at the station. You start up your words again and give them to me; you speak with that voice of yours, so much softer than the one that uttered your no, your refusal. You use it just for me. I'm the only one who hears it. I curl up inside it, and also in your smell, your special smell, which carries a hint of apprehension. I wonder how you cope with it all, the worries about sugar levels, the complex treatment, the constant vigilance, the worry and pain of your failing kidneys. Your smell struck me when I opened the car door to let you in, and I felt embarrassed. I hadn't noticed it at the wedding. It was more spacious there, more ventilated, and less time had passed. There was still fresh perfume in the air. And you hadn't worked yourself up into a state by saying no. You were just out of place. Out of place and all over the place, trying to get into the photo in front of the church, smiling and laughing. We're closer to the evening now, closer to being tired, in a fug of lingering smells and resentment. You're talking calmly to me, saying goodbye and thank you. I've got used to your smell. After paying for your train ticket I give you a hug. You say thank you so many times.

I get back on the road and I don't know if I'll be able to return to the venue, my make-up smudged after all the emotion, ugly with shame, hair wild, so upset that I feel cracked, separate, a stranger, a stranger in my own family. I've got your smell on me. I hope no one will ask any questions and I hope no one will talk about you. I'll open the door and try to conceal my dishevelled looks and my turmoil behind a smile. I'll sit down surreptitiously amid a strange silence, a perplexed halt in the conversation, at the empty space by the little card bearing your name.

# 13

## *Glitter*

It doesn't do the pages any good, or my skin, or the binding, or my veins, or the environment, but I can't resist: I read in the bath, stretched out, luxuriating, late in the evening. Interminable baths and books with lots of foam, steam, fizzing, tension and darkness. Very hot baths and icy books; softly lit baths with scented candles all around, and dark, nauseating books. Sad, turbid stories told with violence and precision. Perfumed water, warm and comfortable.

Really I should feel guilty because, most of the time, they're not even my own books but ones I've borrowed from the city library. So as not to feel bad, I used to tell myself that at least someone was reading them, even if they were getting wrinkled and tatty.

I thought the books were rather neglected, given the librarians' silent astonishment when I went up to the desk. When I returned them, a little damp and scented, I thought there wouldn't be many readers who'd mind.

People see these books as difficult and demanding, discouragingly long and imposing. They're full of wild sentences that I think I can tame with bubbles, warm water and a few drops of essential oil carried in the steam. I inhale the steam, and the sentences come in through my eyes, everything mingling in my brain almost before I realize. I open my head and my legs, and the water surges around the words. My skin softens and words penetrate me. Sometimes a smidgeon of ink comes off on my fingers. I peel away parts of words or commas. It hurts my skin a little and I suck the painful spot absent-mindedly. And I listen. With my body in the water the words become sonorous. I hear them better and sometimes I even touch them. Once they're tamed, assimilated, the books remain inside my body. I get out of the bath and dry myself, and I'm a new woman. I put the book down near my towel and I'm a rich woman. The books on the tiled floor prop me up like stakes, then germinate and ferment on this frame, clinging, distilling themselves. There are stalks, nuts and bolts around my bones and in my head, making me stronger, solidifying me.

It's the opposite for some of my girlfriends. They read standing up, squashed and tense in the dirt and noise of the metro, and their books are warm and easy, so light you can see the fabric of the story as you flick through the pages. They're sparkly books, full of obvious symbols and sweet-smelling words, books you can't get lost in, that never really get under your skin. These are books that leave my friends tired and lethargic, that they forget as soon as they take a shower. Still standing up.

Limp, shiny books, with garish golden or silvery covers. Masks.

These readers are still grimy from the day, on their way home from work with a book in one hand, the other grasping a bar or a hanging strap. They hope to find something in these sickly-sweet pages to help them forget their dirty lives, but it doesn't work. For a book to change us, to cleanse us, it must get deep inside, and those pink books, as I've told them hundreds of times, stay on the surface. They reach only the outer layers of our skin, our thoughts and memories. They smooth over worries with illusory balm, like the anti-wrinkle creams that my friends spread on their faces. All those creams do is make the skin swell up, attacking and irritating it, a lie that they mistake for alleviation. It's just a temporary inflammation hiding the wrinkles. Puffy, that's what my friends are.

I've got lots of wrinkles around my eyes and mouth, from reading and laughing, and for me those wrinkles are the traces of my life, my fun. I'm alive and I read real books. Not dead books that simply submit to being read.

I'm alive, and I read, but I'm not the only one who reads those books, as I used to believe so proudly.

One evening the steam from my bath helped me to pull apart the pages of a book that had got stuck together in some kind of domestic mishap. I was very curious about this mishap. So it wasn't just one damp, languishing person who read these sorts of books, there were also clumsy oafs leaving patches of who knows what all over the pages. I was genuinely surprised, because I really thought I was the only person who'd read that particular book, its only reader, a rare, exceptional reader, blah blah blah. I couldn't completely free the pages that the steam had begun to separate so I stretched up to reach a nail file on the shelf above the sink. The water sloshed noisily from my body and I let it fall from my breasts and thighs as I tried to concentrate on forcing open the still-resistant pages. I sat back down in the bath with my little tool and finally managed to detach the two pages. A multicoloured cloud rose from the sentences and settled in a thin layer on the bubbly surface of the cooling bathwater. Glitter. Dried-up sticky glitter, like the stuff you find in tubes decorated with hearts inside little girls' pencil cases. Girly glitter between the most violent, disturbing and dark pages of this impossible book. Glitter like the stuff on the covers of the books my friends read.

I went to the library the very next day and began looking at people's hands. I was obsessed. I stared unashamedly at hands resting on the issue desk, writing at the tables, holding newspapers, opening books, coming out of pockets. I wasn't looking at the books any more, but at people's hands holding the books, searching for glitter. Searching for readers. I was looking for evidence of other people reading my books.

I didn't find any little-girl glitter, just a very dignified gentleman striking a childish pose, holding a classic novel in one hand and sucking the thumb of the other. Seeing my curious glance, he held up his injury by way of explanation: a cut on his thumb from opening the book's dry pages. A little cut from a clumsy manoeuvre made a man resemble a small child.

I found all sorts of touching signs like this one. I saw hands of every size, and noticed how varied the colour and texture of the skin were. But no proof of reading on them, except that sucking of a tiny cut made by pages read too much, or not enough.

I stopped observing readers' hands. I realized that I just needed to read and read and read, even more library books. That way I'd find proof hidden in the pages themselves, as long as I could read differently, read for tiny clues, like looking for Wally.

Now I knew that when I filled my bag with all the books I'd borrowed, I was also borrowing traces of lives. Traces of other people's reading and, with them, little pieces of their lives, their lives at the moment of their reading, their lives shortly before.

I don't just read the lives of my books' characters any more, I also read the lives of the people reading the stories. When I borrow books, I take with me glimpses of their daily goings-on, all the little doings that fill our own stories and mingle with those in the books, sometimes to the extent of leaving their marks on the pages, the inside things and the outside things. A squashed fly, a feather marking a page, tiny pieces of bread, still fresh, or stale old breadcrumbs.

I never did find more glitter. But I found readers. I've found other proofs of reading. I'm no longer alone reading these demanding books, no longer alone in my steamy bath, my bubble.

I've found pages gummed with all sorts of improbable glues and stained with dozens of unexpected substances: chocolate goo, coffee spills, shiny glue blobs, flecks of brownish dried blood, the scent of soap, pearly slicks of nail varnish. And I'm still discovering.

## TRANSLATORS' NOTE

As always when we translate Emmanuelle Pagano's work, our process has been to divide the initial labour, then to swap drafts and edit and critique, then to swap and go through again, then to swap again and again until neither we nor, we hope, anyone else can say whose half is whose. This is truly a co-translation.

If you compare *Faces on the Tip of My Tongue* with its original French text, *Un renard à mains nues* ('A Fox with My Bare Hands' – both titles emerge out of key phrases in the stories), you will notice that the English book is shorter. We have collaborated with Emmanuelle to make a selection for this English edition that focuses on and brings out the connections between the stories. There are many connections in the original book, some on the surface and others more deeply hidden, some as slight as a repeated sound or word, others as insistent as a recurring character, but we have privileged those that add up to fuller stories in themselves and point to fuller relationships between the characters. We have added nothing but this more deliberate emphasis.

And considering those characters, it seems worthwhile to anticipate a criticism that may come easily in times newly – and appropriately – sensitive to questions of minority experience. We use the word 'loony' on several occasions, including in one story's title. We also use nutcase, mad and backward, as well as other terms less directly suggesting mental disturbance and disability. For one thing, Emmanuelle's characters do not mince their words, so we have taken care to reflect their colloquial, raw and ungentle terminology. But also, Emmanuelle frequently describes people who have been rendered marginal by trauma, abandonment, original disability or bad luck, or a mixture of all these things. She honours them with the closeness of her observation, with the care and humour with which she portrays them, and with the honesty with which she conveys the language that surrounds them and contributes to their separateness, their sequestration. It is no accident that there are many roads running through this collection: with roads come barriers and edges, and their inhabitants divide into those who maintain the pace and those who fall by the wayside. The dominant notes here are compassion, connection and wonder; we hope we have done them justice.

JENNIFER HIGGINS AND SOPHIE LEWIS

# Subscribe

Discover the best of contemporary European literature: subscribe to Peirene Press and receive a world-class novella from us three times a year, direct to your door. The books are sent out six weeks before they are available in bookshops and online.

Your subscription will allow us to plan ahead with confidence and help us to continue to introduce English readers to the joy of new foreign literature for many years to come.

| *'A class act.'* GUARDIAN

| *'Two-hour books to be devoured in a single sitting: literary cinema for those fatigued by film.'*
| TIMES LITERARY SUPPLEMENT

A one-year subscription costs £35 (3 books, free p&p for UK)

Please sign up via our online shop at www.peirenepress.com/shop

## BASMEH & ZEITOONEH
### RELIEF & DEVELOPMENT

Peirene is proud to support Basmeh & Zeitooneh.

Basmeh & Zeitooneh (The Smile & The Olive) is a Lebanese-registered NGO. It was established in 2012 in response to the Syrian refugee crisis. B&Z aims to create opportunities for refugees to move beyond being victims of conflict and help them to become empowered individuals who one day will return to their own country to rebuild their society. Today the organization is managing nine community centres in the region: seven in Lebanon and two in Turkey.

Peirene will donate 50p from the sale of this book to the charity. Thank you for buying this book.

www.basmeh-zeitooneh.org